"Are you flirting with me?" Summer asked.

For months, Kyle had felt as if a spring had been coiled too tight inside him. This woman was slowly unwinding him. She'd taken a chance when she'd opened her door last night. Maybe she kept Mace under the counter. If she had a stun gun, she hadn't needed it. He'd felt hypnotized at first sight.

"If I were flirting with you," he said huskily, "you'd know it."

"It's not every day a girl meets an honest man."

And then she did something for which there was no turning back. She smiled as if she meant it.

Kyle couldn't help reaching for her any more than he could help drawing his next breath. He covered her mouth with his before either of them thought to resist.

Dear Reader,

As I write this letter, a song about going home again is playing on the radio. The lyrics call to me, for a few years ago my childhood home was nearly destroyed in a fire. By some lovely miracle, my parents got out alive.

Recently I had the pleasure of watching them as they celebrated a milestone anniversary. When asked to share the secret for such a long and successful marriage, my soft-spoken mother said, "Divorce, never. Murder, maybe."

Ah, the stuff of good old fairy tales. It's safe to say I came by my sense of humor and my determination naturally.

My parents couldn't go home again after the fire, but I invite you to step into that feeling of homecoming with me as you begin my new series, Round-the-Clock Brides. Turn the page to read *A Bride Until Midnight*....

I hope you love every word.

Welcome home,

Sandra Steffen

A BRIDE UNTIL MIDNIGHT

SANDRA STEFFEN

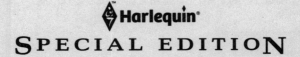

Harlequin®

SPECIAL EDITION

Recycling programs
for this product may
not exist in your area.

ISBN-13: 978-0-373-65593-9

A BRIDE UNTIL MIDNIGHT

Books by Sandra Steffen

SANDRA STEFFEN

is an award winning, bestselling author of more than thirty-seven published novels. Honored to have won the RITA® Award, the National Readers' Choice Award and the Wish award, her most cherished regards come from readers around the world. After growing up in an idyllic setting that inspired her to write at a young age, Sandra married and soon had four little boys while simultaneously pursuing her dream of publication. Her sons have grown up and blessed her with four beautiful daughters-in-law and seven precious grandbabies (so far). These days she is thoroughly enjoying balancing writing, bottle-feeding and travel.

For Denis & Mary Lou Rademacher,
two of the finest role models and
well-loved parents in the world.

Chapter One

Sheet lightning flirted with the treetops on the horizon as Innkeeper Summer Matthews started up the sidewalk of her inn. For a few seconds she could see the bridge over the river and the steeple of the tallest church in Orchard Hill. An instant later the starless sky was black again.

Directly ahead of her, The Orchard Inn beckoned. Nestled on a hill overlooking the river, the inn was just inside the Orchard Hill city limits. Built of sandstone and river rock, it was tall and angular and had a roof that looked like a top hat from here. The large windows, wide front walkway and ornate portico were welcoming. A single antique lamp glowed in the bay window on the first floor. Upstairs the flicker of laptops and televisions, modern technology in a 120-year-old inn, cast a blue haze on the wavy window panes.

Only one window remained dark.

Summer went in through the front door, the purling of the bell blending with the lively voices of her friends who were watching the front desk in her absence. She listened at the stairs for guests and checked the registration book on her way by. K. Miller, the last member of the restoration crew scheduled to begin work on the train depot first thing in the morning, still hadn't checked in. Wondering what was keeping him, she followed her friends' voices to her private quarters.

"You're home early." Madeline Sullivan, whose surprise engagement to Riley Merrick was the reason for tonight's emergency wedding-planning session, was the first to notice Summer. Madeline's blue eyes shone with newfound joy.

Chelsea Reynolds looked up from her laptop, and Abby Fitzpatrick turned in her chair.

Giving Summer a quick once over from head to toe, Abby said, "I saw the new veterinarian getting into his truck with roses and a bottle of wine. And you wore a dress, which means you shaved your legs. What are you doing home already?"

Summer went to the refrigerator for a Diet Coke before joining the others at her table. "Did you know that goats, when born, land on only three feet?"

There was a moment of silence while the others searched for the relevance in that little pearl of wisdom.

"Goats," Abby repeated as Chelsea deftly plucked a blade of straw from Summer's light brown hair.

"Do you have experience birthing goats?" Madeline asked.

"I do now." She popped the top of her soda can and poured the cold beverage into a glass. "Nathan's service called during dinner. One of the Jenkins's goats was struggling to deliver. I went along on the emergency house call. The twins are fine, and the mother is resting, but I definitely shaved my legs for nothing."

Madeline was a nurse whose blond hair and blue eyes gave her an angelic appearance. Blond, too, Abby wore her hair in a short, wispy style that suited her petite frame but camouflaged an IQ that rivaled Einstein's. Chelsea had dark brown hair, a curvy build and a no-nonsense attitude. All three of her friends burst out laughing, and Summer couldn't help joining in.

Looking at these women sitting around her table on this quiet Tuesday night, it occurred to her that when she'd arrived in Orchard Hill six years ago at the tender age of twenty-three, she'd been as fragile and wobbly as one of the Jenkins's newborn goats. Madeline, Chelsea and Abby had befriended her, and in doing so, they'd held her up until she'd gotten both feet firmly underneath her. A year and a half ago, they'd all done the same for Madeline when her fiancé was tragically killed in a motorcycle accident. Now Madeline was standing on her own again, about to be married to the man who'd received Aaron's heart.

"How are the wedding plans coming?" Summer asked.

"Amazing," Abby said. "In ten days the most miraculous wedding of the century will go down in history right here in Orchard Hill."

Summer wished Abby hadn't worded it exactly that way. She *wanted* Madeline's wedding to be a dream come true—nobody deserved this happiness more—but a wedding that went down in history would undoubtedly be high profile. The thought of *that* sent dread to the pit of her stomach.

She reminded herself that most people harbored a profound desire to be remembered for something, to leave their mark on the world. At the very least they wanted their elusive five minutes of fame.

Not Summer.

She'd already made her splash and a messy one at that. Not that anyone in Orchard Hill knew the melodramatic details of her former life. As much as she loved this town and the life she'd found here, she preferred her little secret to remain just that. Hers.

"I think we've done all we can do until morning," Chelsea said. The official wedding planner, she closed her laptop.

The others gathered up their things, too.

Leading the little entourage out the door, Chelsea said, "We have the church, the reception hall, the caterers, the gown and the guest list. We still have to talk about music, flowers, table favors and Madeline's vows, but we're in good shape. Don't you agree, Madeline?"

Summer wondered when Chelsea would notice that Madeline wasn't listening. She wasn't even following anymore. She'd stopped in the center of the courtyard and, as she often did, lifted her face to the dark sky.

"I want apple blossoms on the altar and no gifts," she said. "I want a simple wedding."

From across the courtyard, Chelsea said, "Apple blossoms on the altar will be lovely, and we can request no gifts. But a simple wedding with three hundred guests?"

"Two-hundred-ninety-eight," Madeline said, blinking up at the starless sky. "Riley spoke with his brothers. They don't see how they can possibly get out of their commitments on such short notice. They'll both be out of the country for the wedding."

"Two of the most eligible bachelors on the guest list aren't coming?" Abby asked.

"Shoot," Chelsea said at the same time.

It was all Summer could do to keep the relief from bubbling out of her. Kyle Merrick was Riley's older brother and had grown up in Bay City on Michigan's gold coast. He'd caused quite a stir when he'd gotten kicked out of his Ivy League college, but it was his exposé of a professor's wrongdoing that gained him real notoriety. He'd accepted the formal apology from the university but turned his nose up at their invitation to return. With an attitude like his, it wasn't surprising he'd become a nationally acclaimed journalist. As a newspaperman, he'd likely caught her exclusive the day she'd made the front page of the society section of every major newspaper on the eastern seaboard.

He wasn't coming to his brother's wedding. Summer couldn't contain her happiness about that. It was all she could do to keep from performing cartwheels across the courtyard.

"Before you go," Madeline called. "I want all three of you to close your eyes."

Abby was the first to do as Madeline asked. Although Chelsea complained, she closed her eyes, too. Summer was still smiling when she finally acquiesced.

"Take a deep breath," Madeline continued in her quiet, lilting voice that for a moment seemed almost otherworldly. "Now, slowly release it and draw in another. Relax. Breathe. With your eyes closed, picture the man of your dreams. Do you see him? Maybe he's rugged and moody, or shirtless and sexy, or brainy and pensive."

An image sauntered unbidden across Summer's mind. No matter how many dates she accepted, or how much she enjoyed the attention of the rugged, earthy men of Orchard Hill, her fantasy man wasn't clad in faded jeans or chinos. He was loosening the button on a fine European suit.

Champagne taste on a beer budget.

"Believe your paths will cross, and they will," Madeline said. "I'm living proof. Now open your eyes."

All four of them opened their eyes at the same time. They were still blinking when lightning flashed across the horizon. As if in answer, the lights in the inn flickered.

"The universe just sent us a sign," Madeline whispered in awe. "Your lover is on his way."

Summer didn't know if Chelsea and Abby believed in Madeline's prediction, but they got in Chelsea's car without disputing it. Madeline had always been intuitive and romantic. Since she'd discovered wealthy architect

Riley Merrick and had proceeded to fall in love with him, she'd become even more wise and serene. She believed in destiny and positive thoughts manifesting into positive results. And she believed the flickering lights were a sign.

Summer believed in the cantankerous electrical system in her inn. If that storm came any closer, a fuse would blow, and her lights would go out. There was nothing magical about it, she thought, after Madeline left, too. And the balmy breeze fluttering the loose gathers in her dress's bodice *wasn't* a prelude to a lover's touch.

It was just the wind.

Tall and muscular, the man crossing Summer's threshold watched her watching him. Although she couldn't see his eyes clearly, she saw his bold smile.

Bold with a capital B.

There were times when a woman didn't appreciate such over-confidence. This wasn't one of them.

His chest was bare. Why, she didn't know. He didn't seem to care that he was dripping on an impeccably tailored, white shirt lying on the floor. He kicked it aside with the toe of one worn boot. Summer knew there was something incongruous about his attire, but this was her dream, and she was enjoying it too much to rouse herself enough to analyze the inconsistencies.

Thunder rolled, ever closer, the sound moving through the darkness, approaching as rhythmically and steadily as the man. And what a man—a long, lean paradigm of natural elegance, honed muscle and masculine intent.

Apparently unaffected by the fury of the storm, he smiled as he leaned over her. She held her breath as she waited to be awakened with his kiss.

Thunder cracked right outside the window, and Summer jerked awake. She blinked. Floundered.

Where was she?

Rain pelted the windowpanes, and thunder rumbled again. As she ran her hand over the cushion beside her, her memory gradually returned. She'd curled her feet underneath her at one corner of the settee in the central foyer to wait for the last guest to arrive. She must have fallen asleep. Had she been dreaming? The details of the fantasy escaped her, but there was a yearning in her belly that reminded her how long it had been since she'd known a lover's touch.

Darn Madeline and her silly predictions.

Summer squinted into the darkness. Darkness?

The lights had been on when she'd curled up with her magazine. The power must have gone out. Luckily she'd anticipated the likelihood of that and had put her candle lighter and hurricane lamp on the registration counter soon after Madeline, Chelsea and Abby left.

Now that she had her bearings, she padded barefoot to the desk where she easily located the lighter and removed the glass chimney from the hurricane lamp. She was in the process of lighting the wick when a fist pounded the door behind her.

She spun around, the lighter still flaming. Lightning blazed across the sky just then, outlining the dark figure of a man on her portico.

She reeled backwards.

"I'm here for the room," he said, water sluicing off his rain slicker.

K. Miller, the missing carpenter, she thought. Of course.

With her heart still racing, she took her finger off the lighter's trigger then turned down the wick of the lamp. "The power's out," she called, after replacing the globe.

"It went out with that last streak of lightning as I was pulling in," he said loudly enough to be heard through her front door. "I don't need electricity. All I need is a dry corner to crash until morning."

She unlocked the door. Leaving him space to enter, she slipped behind the counter where she normally greeted guests.

There was something oddly familiar about the way he stepped over the threshold. Which was strange, because she was sure she didn't know him.

Wet, his hair was the color of her favorite coffee, dark and rich and thick. His eyebrows were straight and slightly lighter than his hair, his eyes too shadowed for her to discern their color from here. A drop of water trailed down his cheek before getting caught on the whisker stubble darkening his jaw. He hung his jacket on the coat tree next to the door then started toward the desk.

Green. His eyes were green and so deep they shot a bolt of electricity straight through her. The atmosphere in the room thickened—desire at first sight. He must have felt it, too, because he wasn't moving anymore, either.

"Are you the innkeeper?" he finally asked, dropping his duffel bag at his feet.

"Summer Matthews, yes. Welcome to The Orchard Inn."

Maybe it was the lamplight. Maybe it was the late hour and the rain, but her voice sounded throatier and somehow sultrier in her own ears. If one of them didn't put an end to this soon, clothes were going to start falling off.

"Everyone else arrived hours ago," she said, taking a stab at normalcy.

He delved into his back pocket. It took her a little longer than usual to realize that he was probably fishing for his credit card so he could register.

She pushed the leather-bound book toward him and said, "As long as the power is out, my computer is, too. If you'd just sign the registry, we can settle up in the morning."

He hurriedly wrote his name. Leaving the book open on the other side of the counter, he turned his attention back to her. That delicious warmth uncurled deep inside her again.

Well well well. Here she was having sexy thoughts about a rugged, earthy man who definitely was not wearing a two-hundred-dollar tie. There was hope for her yet.

"You're in Room Seven." She handed him a key, since the electronic key card wouldn't work during a power outage, the number seven dangling from a metal ring. "Upstairs, to your right, then all the way to the end of the hall."

He accepted the key and her venture back to decorum without saying a word. After picking up his duffel bag, he headed for the stairs.

"Wait," she called.

He turned around slowly, his gaze steady and bold. Bold with a capital B.

Outside, thunder rumbled. Inside, lamplight flickered like temptation.

"Yes?" he asked.

"You'll need this flashlight."

He wrapped his fingers around one end of the light. The logical corner of her brain that was still functioning knew she was supposed to release her end now, but she couldn't seem to do more than tip her head back and look at him.

He was handsome but not in a classical way. His features were too rugged for that, his jaw darkened with beard stubble and damp from the rain. His face was lean and angular, forehead, cheekbones, chin; his lips were just full enough to cause a woman to look twice. There was a small scar below his nose, but it was his eyes that caused a ripple to go through her. Something about him brought out a yearning to hold and be held, to touch and be touched.

He must have felt it, too, because his gaze delved hers before dropping to her mouth. From there, it was a natural progression to her shoulders, bared by her sleeveless dress, and finally to the V that skimmed the upper swells of her breasts.

He drew a slow breath, and it was as if they were both suspended, on the brink of taking the next step.

If either of them made the slightest movement, be it a gentle sway or the hint of a smile, there would be no turning back.

She finally garnered the wherewithal to release the flashlight and step away. Giving herself a mental shake, she said, "I hope you enjoy your stay at the inn. Good night, Mr. Miller."

She'd surprised him. No doubt a man with his masculine appeal was accustomed to a different outcome. But he didn't press her. Instead, he turned the flashlight on and followed the beam of light up the stairs.

"It's not Miller," he said, halfway to the top.

"Pardon me?" she asked.

"My name isn't Miller. It's Merrick. Kyle Merrick."

The thud of his footsteps had quieted, and his door had closed before Summer moved. Looking dazedly around the room, her gaze finally fell upon the open registration book. She ran to it and spun it around. By the light of the oil lamp she read the bold scrawl.

Kyle Merrick.

Oh no.

A few hours ago Madeline had said that neither of Riley's brothers was planning to attend the wedding. So what was Kyle doing here?

Regardless of his reasons, the wealthy, world-renowned journalist with a nose for scandal and a penchant for stirring up trouble was spending the night right upstairs, and it was too late for Summer to do anything about it.

The Merricks were self-made millionaires. The jacket hanging on the coat rack was likely made in Italy. Kyle probably owned a closet full of European suits. No matter how far she'd thought she'd come these past six years, her taste in men hadn't changed.

She'd been wildly attracted to him and had come very close to succumbing to the desire he brought out in her. There was no other way to describe the awareness that had arced between them. She couldn't explain it, and she couldn't deny that she'd felt it. A delicious current lingered even now. She had little doubt an attraction like that would have led to more passion than she'd experienced in a long time.

But he was Kyle Merrick.

And she was…well, Summer wasn't her given name.

Chapter Two

Kyle Merrick's Jeep Wrangler was equipped with the most advanced navigational system on the market, but he rarely turned it on. Relying on technology dulled a man's natural instincts. Besides, it was more fun to use the sense of direction he'd been born with. It came in handy when he needed to find a way out of dicey situations in some of the world's largest cities, poorest villages and, on occasion, women's hotel rooms.

Locating the house where his brother was staying didn't require navigational gadgetry, carefully honed skill or God-given talent. Once Kyle had narrowed it down to the general vicinity—east of the river and north of Village Street—Riley's silver Porsche in the driveway had been impossible to miss.

Kyle parked the Jeep and got out. As he sauntered to the door, he noted his surroundings, something else that came naturally. This neighborhood was in an old section of Orchard Hill, but, unlike the residences on the national historic registry, the houses here were small and nondescript. This bungalow wasn't Riley's type of house at all. Which meant it was Madeline Sullivan's.

Since there was no sense putting off the inevitable, he raised his fist and knocked on the door. A large, brown dog bounded outside the instant the door was opened.

While the dog took care of business on an unsuspecting hedge, the Merrick brothers faced one another, each carefully assessing the other.

Riley was the first to speak. "I wondered which one of you The Sources would send."

Kyle grimaced because this *did* feel a little like a mission. He'd wanted Braden to come but had lost the toss.

He and his brothers had a father in common and three separate mothers. It accounted for the similarities in their height and build and the differences in their eye colors and personalities. They hadn't always gotten along, but they'd always been a united front when it came to their mothers, otherwise known as The Sources. In this instance, Kyle didn't blame them for being concerned about Riley's recent, hasty engagement.

Apparently Riley understood that this confrontation was inevitable. He threw the door wide and said, "You might as well come in."

Kyle and the dog followed him through a comfortably furnished living room where blueprints were spread across a low table and a fax was coming in. They ended up in a yellow kitchen where a television droned and steam rose from a state-of-the-art coffeemaker.

Catching Kyle looking around, Riley said, "She's not here."

Instead of offering Kyle a seat at the table, Riley leaned against the counter and took a sip from one of the mugs he'd just filled. There was no delicate way to do this, and they both knew it. They also both knew that Kyle wouldn't leave until he'd had his say.

Carrying his coffee to a spot that was a safe distance from his brother, Kyle leaned a hip against the counter, too, and said, "You can't blame us for being concerned. Two years ago, you were dying. Two months ago, you still weren't yourself. Now you're getting married in a week and a half to a woman you proposed to after you'd known her a matter of days."

"Don't form an opinion until you've met Madeline."

"I'm sure she's a saint. I heard she was wearing your sheet the first time she met your mother." Kyle wouldn't have minded being a fly on that wall, but Riley didn't share the details of the encounter. Merrick men didn't kiss and tell.

"You have to admit it looks suspicious," Kyle said. "She's a nurse. You have money."

"Madeline doesn't care about money."

Everybody cared about money. But Kyle said, "She showed up uninvited at one of your construction sites, and she failed to mention that the heart beating in your chest came from her deceased fiancé."

"Water under the bridge," Riley insisted before taking another sip of coffee.

Following suit, Kyle said, "You fell for her. Hard. I get that. So live with her for a while. Make sure the penny doesn't lose its shine."

"I'm marrying her, Kyle, the sooner, the better."

The dog stood up and looked from one to the other.

"What's your hurry?" Kyle asked. "It's not as if you *have* to marry her." He stopped. The drone of the television covered an uncomfortable lag in conversation. "Is that what this is about? She's pregnant?"

Riley shot him a warning look.

And Kyle muttered the only word that came to mind.

"We're not telling anyone yet," Riley said. "So keep it to yourself. I don't know what I did to deserve Madeline, to deserve any of this, but whatever it was, I'm not wasting another minute of my life without her."

Kyle fought the urge to rake his fingers through his hair. "You slept with her, and now she claims she's going to have your baby. Don't hit me for what I'm thinking."

He could tell Riley wanted to hit him. It wouldn't be a sucker punch, either. Riley didn't fight dirty, but he fought to win, something else the Merrick men had in common.

"Have you ever *known* a virgin, Kyle?" he asked.

It took a few seconds for Riley's meaning to soak in. "You mean Madeline? For real? You're sure?"

"Positive."

Kyle put his coffee down. "I'll be damned. A virgin.

I didn't know there were any alive past the age of eighteen. Make that seventeen. Fine. The kid's yours. That's good. I guess. I'm just saying—"

"You're saying it's all happening fast and you, Braden and our mothers are worried about that. I trust you'll put their minds at ease. In your own good time, of course."

They shared their first smile. Riley knew him well.

"Anything else you'd like me to tell our mothers?" Kyle asked, suddenly not at all sorry he'd lost that toss to Braden.

"Tell them I can feel my heart beating."

This time Kyle didn't say anything. He simply stared in amazement at his younger brother.

He would never forget the panic and paralyzing fear that had ripped through the entire family twenty months ago when they'd learned that Riley had contracted a rare virus that was attacking his heart. In a matter of days, he'd gone from strong and athletic to wan and weak. He was only thirty years old. And he was dying.

Kyle, Braden and Riley's friend Kipp had stayed with him around the clock. They'd begged him, badgered him and bullied him to hold on. Two years younger than Kyle, Riley had been at death's door, literally, by the time he'd finally received a heart transplant. His recovery had been nothing short of a miracle, but, despite his robust health afterwards, there had been something different about him. It was as if his sense of adventure, his passion and even his laughter had been buried with his old heart. Strangely, he hadn't been able to feel the new one beating.

"How long has the feeling been back?" Kyle asked.

"Since Madeline." Riley placed a hand over his chest. "I used to climb mountains just for the view from the top. That view is nothing compared to what I see when I look into her eyes. I can see the future, and that's never happened to me before."

Kyle held up one hand. He didn't know how much more he could take on an empty stomach.

Riley laughed. And for a moment it took Kyle back to summer vacations and boyhood pranks they'd pulled together. He hadn't heard Riley laugh quite like this in a long time. It did Kyle's heart good.

"I'll tell The Sources you're happy and as healthy as the proverbial horse and I'll tell them you can feel your beating heart. I'm glad, man. It's good to see you. Real good. Now, I have a plane to catch to L.A."

He was already out the door when Riley said, "You look good, too, Kyle. More rested than I expected."

The brothers shared a long look, Kyle in the watery rays of late morning sunshine and Riley in the shadow of the doorway. If they were keeping score, this point would go to Riley, for, with his simple statement, he'd let Kyle know that Riley wasn't the only one their mothers were worried about. Kyle hadn't been himself lately, either. He was going through something. Running from something.

The Sources worked both ways.

"If I look rested," Kyle said, "it's because I slept like a baby last night."

"During that storm?"

Kyle couldn't explain it, but once he'd closed his eyes,

he hadn't heard a thing for nine solid hours. The inn had been empty and the power was back on by the time he'd wandered downstairs this morning. Now, standing in a patch of sunshine beneath his brother's watchful gaze, he found himself thinking about the woman with the large, hazel eyes and sultry, cultured voice that made hello sound like an intimate secret.

"Can your plane ride wait until after lunch?" Riley asked.

"That depends. Are you cooking?"

Again, the brothers shared a grin.

Riley, who often burned toast, said, "I thought I'd call Madeline at work and see if she can join us at the restaurant downtown. I'd like you to meet her."

"Let me know what time," Kyle said as he climbed into his Jeep.

Meanwhile, he had a woman to see about a room.

Robins splashed in the puddles in the inn's driveway as Summer pulled into her usual parking place. She lifted her cloth bags from her trunk and started toward the backdoor, the groceries in her arms growing heavier with every step she took. The sound of Kyle Merrick's deep voice coming through the kitchen window sent the headache she'd awakened with straight to the roots of her teeth.

She'd spent the first half of the night tossing and turning, her body yearning to finish what meeting Kyle Merrick had started. Between short bursts of fitful sleep, she'd lain awake staring at the dark ceiling, anticipating the hate mail she would receive from the people she'd duped should her secret ever be revealed.

Her father, for one. Her former fiancé, for another.

Sometimes she imagined her mother and sister sitting on a cloud, smiling down at her and singing a song about sweet revenge. To this day, she knew she'd done the right thing. That didn't mean she wanted to relive what was to have been her wedding day.

She heard Kyle's voice again. This time it was followed by a flirtatious, though aging, twitter Summer would recognize anywhere. Harriet Ferris lived next door and was always happy to watch the front desk when Summer needed to run errands during the day. Harriet told raucous stories and loved nothing better than having a captive audience, especially if it was someone of the opposite sex.

Summer almost felt sorry for Kyle.

Almost.

What was he doing in the inn, anyway?

He'd gone. She'd freshened the rooms after breakfast and made the beds. Room Seven had been empty. She'd checked.

Kyle Merrick's duffel bag was gone. And she'd been relieved. Okay, she'd felt a little unsettled, too, but that was beside the point.

For some reason he was back—she had no idea why—and was sitting at the table, no doubt sharing raucous tales with Summer's next-door neighbor. He looked up at her as she walked in and almost smiled.

"I thought you'd left," she said.

"Without paying for my stay last night? Your low opinion of me is humbling."

He didn't look humble. He looked like a man with sex on his mind, the kind of man who didn't ask for commitment and certainly didn't give it. Lord-a-mighty, the invitation in those green eyes was tempting.

"What makes you think I've formed an opinion about you?" she asked.

He smiled, and the connection between their gazes thrummed like a guitar string being strummed with one finger. Pulling her gaze from his wasn't easy, but she turned her attention to the woman watching the exchange.

"Would you like a cup of tea, Harriet?"

Seventy-eight-year-old Harriet Ferris had been dying her hair red for fifty years. Before every birthday there was a discussion about letting it go gray, but she never would, just as she would never stop wearing false eyelashes and flirting with men of all ages.

"No, thank you, dear, I really should be getting back home. I'm expecting an email from my sister in Atlanta. She refuses to text. So old-school, you know?"

Although she stood up, she made no move toward the door until Summer leaned down and whispered in her ear.

A smile spread across Harriet's ruby red lips. "What would I do without you? What would any of us do? This handsome man has brought you a gift." Harriet looked from Summer to Kyle and back again. "I won't spoil the surprise, but I dare say if you could bottle the electricity in this room right now, you could sell it to the power company for a tidy profit. If only I were twenty years younger."

"You're a cougar, Harriet," Kyle said, rising, too.

With a playful wink and a grin that never aged, Harriet tottered out the back door.

Now that he and Summer were alone, Kyle handed her the gift bag. "For the next time your power goes out," he said.

She opened the brown paper sack. Peering at the fuses inside, she shook her head and smiled.

He looked like he was about to smile, too, but his gaze caught on her mouth, and Summer knew Harriet was right about the electricity in this room.

"You wanted to settle up for last night's stay?" she asked.

"You aren't from Michigan are you?" he asked.

The question came from out of the blue and caught her by surprise. Years of practice kept her perfectly still, her expression carefully schooled to appear artful and serene.

"I can't place the inflection," he continued. "But it isn't Midwestern."

She pulled herself together. Carrying the milk, eggs and cheese to the refrigerator, she said, "I was born in Philadelphia and grew up in Baltimore. My grandparents had a summer house on Mackinaw Island. Until my grandfather died when I was fourteen, my sister and I spent every summer in northern Michigan. What about you? Where are you from?"

She was just making conversation, for she knew the pertinent facts about his past. She'd researched all three of the Merrick brothers after Madeline had announced her engagement to Kyle's brother Riley a few days ago.

"I was born and raised in Bay City," he said, his voice a lazy baritone that suggested he had all the time in the world. "I studied out east and have traveled just about everywhere else. What did you whisper to Harriet?"

She glanced at him as she closed the refrigerator. "I told her where she put her spare key this week. She keeps moving it and forgets where she hides it."

"Is that why they call you the keeper of secrets?" he asked.

Summer stopped putting away groceries and looked at him. She prided herself on her ability to identify a person's true nature at first sight. She wasn't the only one in this room doing that right now. Kyle was looking at her as if she were a puzzle he had every intention of solving. That felt far more dangerous than the heat in his gaze or the fact that she was wondering if he might kiss her.

She wasn't about to be the first to look away, as if she had something to hide. Which she did, but he didn't know that. And he wouldn't.

Okay. It was time to get both their minds on something else. "Are you flirting with me?" she asked, even though she knew he was.

She could tell her ploy had worked by the change in his stance, the slight tilt of his head, the even slighter narrowing of his gaze. Oh yes, his mind was on something far more fundamental than her past, for nothing was more fundamental than flirting with the opposite sex.

For months, Kyle had felt as if a spring had been coiled too tight inside him. This woman was slowly unwinding him. She'd taken a chance when she'd opened her door last night. Maybe she kept mace under the counter. If she had a stun gun, she hadn't needed it. He'd felt hypnotized at first sight.

Summer Matthews had hazel eyes and curves in all the right places. She was a pretty woman, and he knew his way around pretty women. He didn't understand them, God no, but he knew when a woman wanted what he wanted.

Summer was interested. She just wasn't acting on it. The question was, why? She wasn't wearing a ring, and she was no prude. Nobody with a voice that sultry and a mind that bright was shy and unsure of herself.

She was refreshing and intriguing. Deep inside him, that taut spring unwound a little more.

"If I were flirting with you," he said huskily, "you'd know it."

Her gaze went to his mouth, but instead of continuing the flirtation, she named the amount for last night's stay. His interest climbed another notch, and so did his regard for her.

He liked a woman who could keep her wits about her.

He wished he had enough time to turn those astute eyes starry, to run his hands along her graceful shoulders and feel her arms slowly wind around his neck as her lips parted for his kiss. Unfortunately he was out of time to do more than say, "I'm meeting my brother and future sister-in-law for lunch. After that I have a plane to catch, but I wanted to pay for my room before I leave town."

Pocketing the cash he gave her, she said, "It's not every day a girl meets an honest man."

And then she did something, and there was no turning back. She smiled as if she meant it.

Kyle couldn't help reaching for her any more than he could help drawing his next breath. He covered her mouth with his, before either of them thought to resist.

After that first brush of lips and air, the kiss deepened, breaths mingling, pulse rates climbing. It was a possessive joining, a mating of mouths and heat and hunger. It didn't matter that it was broad daylight, that he had to leave in a few minutes or that he barely knew her. He kissed her because he had to. It was primal, and it was powerful, and, when her mouth opened slightly, he wanted more. He wanted everything.

He'd imagined her body going pliant—he had a damned fine imagination—but it was nothing compared to the reality in his arms. Her hands came around his back, then glided up to his shoulders. She moved against him, and he held her tighter, melding them together from knees to chest.

Somewhere in the back of Summer's mind, warning bells were clanging. She was crazy to be doing this, to be starting something with a man in his field, this man in particular. Doing so was risking discovery. And yet she couldn't seem to help herself. She couldn't stop. She had to experience Kyle's kiss. She needed to know she could feel this way.

Last night when she should have been sleeping, her eyes had been wide open. Now, they closed dreamily, so that she had to rely on her other senses. Her other senses were floating on a serenade of sound, heat and passion.

His mouth was firm and wet, his breathing deep, his scent clean and brisk like mint and leather. The combination made her heart speed up and her thoughts slow like a lazy river on a sultry summer day. His arms and back were muscular, his legs solid and long. It had been a long time since she'd been kissed like this, since she'd reacted like this. Had she ever been kissed quite like this?

Her back arched, her body seeking closer contact even though they couldn't get any closer through their clothes. Until this moment, they'd been strangers. His kiss changed that, and it was spinning out of control. Control was the last thing she wanted, for passion this strong didn't come along every day.

She felt like a balloon held gently between a pair of firm lips, waiting to see if another puff of air would fill her, transforming her, or if those lips would withdraw, sending her careening backwards. The air was Kyle Merrick. Therein lay the risk.

She reminded herself that he was leaving town today, and if she ever saw him again, it would be on rare occasions and only because he was going to be Madeline's brother-in-law. Such meetings would be entirely controllable. It made this feel less dangerous, less likely to be something she would regret. And so, for a few moments, she let herself feel, let herself react, let herself go. And go and go.

For the first time in a long time, she felt like herself. And it felt good.

She felt free.

The kiss didn't end on a need for air. It ended with the sudden jarring and incessant ringing of both their phones.

Hers stopped before she could think clearly enough to answer. It went to voice mail, only to start up again. Whoever was calling was insistent. Kyle's caller was just as determined.

They drew apart, their eyes glazed, mouths wet, breathing ragged. She let her arms fall to her sides. Dazedly, he raked his fingers through his dark hair.

Moving more languidly than usual, as if her hands were having trouble picking up signals from her brain, she finally reached for her cell phone and answered. Normally Summer began speaking the moment she put the phone to her ear. Today, Madeline did that from the other end.

"What?" Summer asked. "Honey, slow down." Although vaguely aware of the low drone of Kyle's voice, too, Summer listened intently to what Madeline was saying. "Of course I'll come. I'll be right there," she said.

Summer was aware that Kyle had pocketed his phone and was watching her. "That was Riley," he said. "I was planning to meet him and Madeline for lunch. He had to cancel."

She glanced at him as she dropped her phone into her bag and fished inside for her keys. "I know. My call was from Madeline."

He watched her, waiting for her to say more. When she didn't, he said, "Riley said it's possible she's losing the baby."

Summer studied his eyes. Only a few people knew Madeline was pregnant. "Riley told you about the baby?"

This time Kyle nodded. "When I saw him this morning, he was happier than I've seen him in a long time."

"Madeline, too," she said quietly.

Summer wanted to shake her fist at fate and demand that this work out for Madeline. She'd already lost so much. Now she'd found Riley, and she was happy. Happy. Was it too much to ask that she could stay that way?

"Dammit all to hell," Kyle said.

Summer wasn't a crier, but tears welled because, for a few moments, she understood. They both felt frustrated and helpless over Madeline's possible medical emergency. Maybe what they said was true. Maybe there was strength in numbers, because she suddenly felt empowered. It went straight to her head. From there, it meandered to places she didn't normally think about in the light of day.

Dresses were her usual work attire. The sleeveless, gray dress she wore today had a fitted waistband and a softly gathered skirt. It wasn't formfitting, yet she was very aware of the places along her body where the lightweight fabric skimmed.

She felt Kyle's gaze move slowly over her, settling momentarily at the little indentation at the base of her neck. It was all she could do to keep from placing her hand where he was looking, for she could feel the soft fluttering of her pulse at her throat. She'd learned to school her expressions, but that little vein had a mind of its own.

Last night, she'd blamed this attraction on the storm. Everybody knew people did crazy things during atmospheric disturbances. Kyle's kiss a few minutes ago had created its own atmospheric disturbance.

But right now, Madeline needed her.

So Summer reeled in her thoughts, tamped down her passion and said, "I don't like to be rude, but I have to go." A handshake seemed a little formal after that kiss, so she settled on a smile. "It was nice meeting you. I mean that. Have a good flight."

Even though it was handled politely, Kyle knew when he was being asked to leave. Since he had no legitimate reason to hang around—he did have a plane to catch after all—he walked out with Summer.

She headed for a blue sedan, and he started toward the lilac hedge in full bloom near where he'd left his Jeep. Pea gravel crunched beneath his shoes. He wasn't sure what made him turn around and look at her. Perhaps it was the same thing that caused her to glance over her shoulder at him at the same time. Whatever the reason, it felt elemental and as fundamental as the pull of a man to a woman and a woman to a man.

Just then, a gust of wind caught in her hair and dress. And it struck him that he'd seen her before.

He knew he was staring, but he couldn't help it. He scanned his memory, trying to identify the reason she seemed familiar.

"Is something wrong?" she asked, obviously in a hurry to be on her way.

Deciding this wasn't the time or place to play twenty questions, he simply said, "No. You have to go. Good luck. Tell Riley I'll be in touch."

She drove away, and he finally got in his Jeep. Instead of starting the engine, he sat behind the steering wheel, thinking. The sensible thing to do would be to turn the key and head for the airport to catch his two o'clock flight to L.A.

Leaving the engine idling, he slipped his laptop from its case and turned it on. He typed Summer's name at the top of his favorite search engine. There were thousands of matches, among them a semi-famous opera singer, a retired drummer from a sixties rock band, and a teacher in Cleveland. There was even a racehorse by that name. Kyle tried another search engine and found an article archived from a local newspaper that listed Summer as the innkeeper of The Orchard Inn.

Minutes later he turned his computer off. Now what?

He wondered what was happening in the Emergency Room. He'd spent days on end at the hospital two years ago when Riley had been so close to death. Riley hadn't asked Kyle to come this time, which was fine with him. Female troubles made all men squeamish. Besides, this was intimate. It was something that was between Riley and Madeline and Madeline's closest friend. That brought Kyle back to Summer.

He was pretty sure he'd never met her. He would have remembered an actual encounter. As he sat strumming his fingers on the armrest, he couldn't shake the feeling that he was missing something.

What?

She hadn't looked familiar until a few moments ago. Did she remind him of someone else? Was that it?

His mind circled around a few possibilities then discarded them. No, she didn't look like anyone he knew. He would have noticed that earlier.

But she was familiar. Although he didn't know where or when, he'd seen her before.

Kyle Merrick never forgot a face.

Chapter Three

The founding fathers of Orchard Hill were an unlikely trio of entrepreneurs from upstate New York. One was said to have been a charming shyster who convinced his business associates back home that wealth awaited them "in the green hills of a promised land."

According to local historians, among the first arrivals were a prominent banker and his wife, who took one look at the crudely built clapboard houses in the village and the surrounding mosquito-infested ramshackle farms and fainted dead away. The second founding father was a botanist who, through much trial and error, developed three species of apples still widely grown in the local orchards today. The third was considered to be a simpleton by his aristocratic parents. This so-called dunce proved to be a man of great wisdom and ambition who eventually established The Orchard Hill Academy, now the University of Orchard Hill.

Historical tidbits were strange things for Summer to be thinking about as she waited at the traffic light at the corner of Jefferson and Elm, but it took her mind off worrying about Madeline or wondering if she'd really glimpsed a momentary recognition in Kyle Merrick's gaze as she was leaving the inn. She gripped the steering wheel and told herself not to jump to conclusions.

He couldn't have recognized her.

It *was* possible he'd seen her photograph in the newspapers six years ago. But she'd been younger then, and blond, and had been wearing a frothy veil and a wedding gown made of acres of silk.

He hadn't recognized her.

How could he? She barely recognized the girl she'd been then.

More than likely, what she'd thought was a fleeting recognition in Kyle's green eyes had simply been a conscious effort to coax the blood back into his brain after that kiss. She pried the fingers of her right hand from the steering wheel and gently touched her lips. He wasn't the only one still recovering.

Enough. They'd enjoyed a brief flirtation. Not mild, mind you, but brief. That was all it was. She had nothing to worry about. He was most likely on his way to the airport this very minute to pursue more pressing stories than a rehash of old news, even if that old news was Baltimore's most notorious runaway bride.

She and Kyle had said their good-byes. Or at least she had. She tried to remember how he'd replied.

"Good luck," he'd said as they'd parted ways. And everybody knew good luck was as good as goodbye.

She jumped when a horn blasted. People in Orchard Hill didn't generally honk their horn, which meant she'd probably been sitting at the green light longer than she should. Smiling apologetically in her rearview mirror at the poor driver behind her, she quickly took her foot off the brake and continued on toward the hospital across town.

Roughly seven square miles, Orchard Hill was a city of nearly twenty-five thousand residents. The streets curved and intersected in undulating juxtaposition to the bends in the river. A state highway bisected the city from east to west, but even that was riddled with stoplights. She'd learned to drive in congested city traffic. She'd learned patience here.

She had to wait a few minutes while a crew wearing hard hats moved a newly fallen tree limb out of the intersection. A few blocks farther down the street a delivery man threw his flashing lights on and left his truck idling in the middle of Division Street. Hosanna chimed from the bell tower as it did every day at half past eleven.

It really was just an ordinary May morning in Orchard Hill. The normalcy of it was like a cool drink of lemonade, refreshing and calming at the same time.

While she waited at another red light she found herself staring at the ten foot tall statue on her left. Nobody could agree where the bronzed figure came from, or how long it had stood on the courthouse lawn.

Summer remembered vividly the first time she'd seen

it more than six years ago. She'd been lost and nearly out of gas that day when she'd coasted to a stop at the curb. So exhausted that the lines and words on the road map in her hand swam before her eyes, she'd found herself gazing out the window at a whimsical figure at the head of a town square.

Most cities reserved a place of such importance for cannons and monuments and statues of decorated war heroes on mighty steeds, but that day she was drawn from her car by a larger-than-life replica of a fellow with holes in his shoes, bowed legs, patched trousers, and a dented kettle on his head. Johnny Appleseed was her first acquaintance in Orchard Hill.

She'd stood beside the statue and taken a deep breath of air scented with ripe apples and autumn leaves. Above the golden treetops in the distance she saw a smoke stack from a small factory, a water tower and several church spires. Somewhere, a marching band was practicing, and there were dog walkers on the sidewalks of what appeared to be a busy downtown.

It had been too early for streetlights, but lamps had glowed in the windows of some of the shops lining the street. Fixing her gaze straight ahead, she'd walked away from her unlocked car, leaving her ATM and credit cards in plain view on the seat inside. A thief wouldn't get far with any of them, for all her cards had been cancelled.

Nobody duped Winston Emerson Matthews the Third without consequences, not even his daughter. Especially not his daughter.

She'd entered the first restaurant she came to and sat

at a small table. A blond waitress a few years younger than Summer had appeared with a menu and a smile. Nearly overtaken with the enormity and finality of her recent actions, Summer stared into the girl's friendly blue eyes and blurted, "Ten days ago I left a rich and powerful man at the altar. My father has disinherited me and all I have left in my purse is ten dollars and some change."

After a moment of quiet deliberation, the waitress had replied, "I'd recommend Roxy's Superman Special." In a whisper, she added, "It's a savory chicken potpie. Roxy makes it from scratch. Her crusts alone could win awards."

Something had passed between their gazes. Summer's eyes filled up, and all she could do was nod.

"I'll be right back." The angelic waitress had soon returned, a plate in each hand. She sat down across from Summer and shook out her napkin. "I'm Madeline Sullivan," she said, handing Summer a fork and napkin and picking up another set for herself. "Welcome to Orchard Hill."

Before the meal was finished, Summer's second acquaintance in Orchard Hill had become the best friend she'd ever known. Madeline had taken Summer home with her, as if normal people took in disinherited young women with secret pasts every day.

She was the only person in Orchard Hill Summer had confided in, the only person who knew her given name.

Madeline had been working her way through college then. Today she was a nurse, and right now she lay in a hospital, possibly losing a baby she desperately wanted.

"I'm coming, Madeline," Summer whispered into the celestial sovereignty reserved for promises and prayers.

Buchanan Street curved one last time before the three-story brick hospital came into view. She followed the arrows and parked near the lighted E.R. sign around back. Grabbing her shoulder bag, she locked her car then ran through the automatic doors and down a short corridor. She rounded a corner.

And came face-to-face with *two* Merrick brothers, not one.

Years of practice with schooling her features very nearly deserted her as she looked from Riley to Kyle. She wanted to ask Kyle what he was doing here. Why wasn't he checking his bag at the airport?

And how had he beaten her here?

Instead she focused on a pair of brown eyes, not green, and said, "Riley, how is she?"

Riley Merrick was as tall as his brother and had a similar build. There was a depth in his eyes that put Summer at ease every time she saw him.

"You know Madeline," he said, his voice a deep baritone. "She keeps telling me not to worry about her, that everything's going to be okay."

That sounded like Madeline.

"What happened?" Summer asked.

"She passed out at work. Hit her head when she fell. The bleeding seems to have stopped."

"She was bleeding?" Summer asked.

"Too heavy to be considered spotting."

Oh. That kind of bleeding. "And the pregnancy?" Summer whispered.

"We're waiting for the results of blood work. A few minutes ago Madeline told me she doesn't *feel* she's lost the baby."

That sounded like Madeline, too.

Apparently Riley realized that Kyle was still standing beside him. He glanced at him, and said, "Summer, this is my brother Kyle."

"Hello, Kyle," she said.

"We meet again," he said at the same time, only slightly louder.

"You two know each other?" Riley asked, looking sideways at his brother.

"Remember when I told you I slept like a baby last night? It was at her place."

"At my *inn*. In Room Seven. Alone. At least I assume he was alone." Summer shot Kyle a stern look before turning back to Riley. "Where is Madeline now?"

Double doors clanked open and a man wearing scrubs pushed a gurney through the doorway. A television droned on the far wall in the waiting area. A little girl was crying, and a teenaged boy was holding his wrist. Other bored-looking people dozed or fidgeted, waiting for their turn to see a doctor.

"She's in Room Four," Riley answered quietly. "Talya's performing an examination."

Talya Ireland, pronounced like Tanya, only with an *l,* was a midwife and Madeline's new employer. She'd stayed at the inn when she first came to town several months ago. If Madeline was with her, she was in good hands.

Summer lowered herself into a nearby vinyl chair. Before she'd even finished smoothing her skirt, Riley said, "Madeline asked me to send you in the minute you arrived."

She was on her feet again and halfway to the door when she thought of something. "Riley?" she said.

Both Merrick brothers were watching her.

"If Madeline feels she's going to be okay," Summer said, "I believe her."

Relief eased the strain on Riley's face. Kyle's expression was more difficult to decipher. He stood looking at her, his shoulders straight, the collar of his shirt open, cuffs rolled to his forearms. He was one of those men who played hard and cleaned up well, and he sent her stomach into a wild swirl. He was ruggedly attractive from the waves in his coffee-colored hair to the toes of his Italian-made shoes.

She forced her eyes away but felt his gaze until she disappeared on the other side of the heavy metal doors. The vinyl flooring beneath her feet muffled the sound of her footsteps. From behind curtain one came the mechanical blip of a heart monitor. Behind curtain two, a child cried forlornly. Hushed voices and a few groans that didn't sound like pain were coming from behind curtain three.

Summer stuck her head inside room four. The hospital bed took up the majority of the narrow cubby; monitors and IV racks competed for space with an efficient-looking midwife.

"Hey," Summer said, drawing Madeline's gaze.

From her pillow, Madeline gave Summer a weak smile. "Hey yourself."

Summer looked at the third woman in the room. In her late thirties, Talya Ireland had exotic gray eyes and five shades of brown hair beauty salons would love to replicate. If there was an ounce of Irish blood in her as her name suggested, it wasn't readily apparent.

While Talya studied the blood pressure printout and fussed with a switch on the IV, Summer sidled closer to the bed and studied Madeline. The two of them were identical in size, yet today Madeline seemed slight and pale and smaller somehow.

"How are you feeling?" Summer asked.

On a shuddering breath, Madeline said, "Oh, Summer. All these sounds and smells and people scurrying around. I used to work here, but this morning all I could think about was the day Aaron died."

Summer took Madeline's hand. Madeline and Aaron Andrews had been childhood sweethearts and inseparable until nearly two years ago when a motorcycle accident cut his life tragically short. Madeline had been with him when he'd taken his last breath in a hospital room similar to this one. It was only natural that the horrors would come back at a time like this.

With a sniffle, Madeline pointed to the thin wall between her room and the room next door, from which came another creak and a muffled moan. "Are they doing what I think they're doing?" she asked.

Nobody could make Summer smile like Madeline.

"Are you blushing?" Madeline asked.

Smoothing the sheet at her patient's waist, Talya said, "Summer is such a lady."

"Take that back." But Summer knew she was smiling again. Friends made life so rich.

"We're talking about you," she said to Madeline. "And you haven't answered my question."

"I'm scared and shaken but better, I think."

Sinking to the edge of the bed, Summer sighed. "You're really okay?"

Madeline nodded. "Talya wants me to stay off my feet for a few days."

"At *least* a few days," came a stern voice from the other side of the bed.

"And the baby?" Summer asked quietly.

"I'm not far enough along to have an ultrasound, but Talya is guardedly optimistic that my pregnancy is still viable and will continue to be so for a good long time."

Talya said, "Sometimes spontaneous bleeding occurs early in a pregnancy. It isn't normal, but it isn't altogether uncommon, either. It's possible her placenta has attached a little low in her uterus. If that's the case, I've seen it spontaneously move up a little to a safer holding place. Right now all we can do is wait and see."

A nurse who used to work with Madeline bustled into the room. "Here's your lab results," she said, handing the report to the midwife. "Hi, Madeline."

Talya read the report. "Your beta levels are elevated. That's a good sign."

The moment she grinned, Summer jumped to her feet. "I'll get Riley."

"I'll go," Talya said. "I like to deliver good news."

With a swish of the curtain, she was gone, only to pop her head through the folds again. "Those sounds coming from your neighbors? Two twelve-year-old girls texting their grandma in Spokane." She made a tsk, tsk, tsk sound with her tongue. "I know what's on your minds." She pointed her finger at Madeline. "None of that for you until I see you again in my office." She winked at Summer. "You are under no restrictions."

An instant later the curtain fluttered back into place. In the ensuing silence, Madeline burst out laughing. It was music to Summer's ears.

"I'll call Chelsea and Abby," Summer said. "We'll contact the caterers, Reverend Brown and everyone on the guest list." Since there hadn't been time to follow normal wedding protocol, most of the invitations went out via email, so it wouldn't be difficult to send another. "We'll tell them the wedding is being postponed for a few weeks."

Madeline was shaking her head. "I want to talk to you about that."

Summer had known Madeline for more than six years. This stubborn streak had begun to emerge *after* she'd discovered newfound happiness with Riley Merrick.

"What is it?" Summer asked.

"I have a favor to ask."

"The answer is yes."

"You haven't heard the request," Madeline insisted.

For years Summer had wanted to repay Madeline in some small or profound way for taking her under her wing when she'd first arrived in Orchard Hill. "No matter what it is, I'll do it." She studied the mischievous glint in Madeline's eyes, another quality that had only recently come out of hiding, and posed her next question more haltingly. "What is the favor?"

Madeline crossed her ankles beneath the sheet, fluffed her pillow and tucked one hand under her head. When she was comfortable, she told Summer what she had in mind.

By the time Talya returned with Riley and Kyle in tow, Summer and Madeline had everything worked out and their plan in place. Summer gave her best friend a warm hug, told Riley goodbye and skirted around Kyle, who still had time, if he hurried, to catch his plane.

She smiled to herself as she walked out into the gorgeous May sunshine. Madeline was right. Everything was going to work out just fine.

Harriet Ferris never did anything halfway.

When Summer returned to the inn, the sassy redhead was talking to a man Summer didn't know. She wore violet today, her slacks, her blouse, her earrings, even the broach on her collar, were a shade of her favorite color. Five feet two in her two-inch purple heels, she rested her elbows on the top of the registration desk and cast Summer a friendly smile. "This is Knox Miller checking in."

The missing K. Miller was here at last.

"Isn't Knox the most masculine name you've ever heard?"

Harriet didn't flirt halfway, either.

It didn't matter that he wore a wedding ring and had

a receding hairline and expanding waist. Harriet didn't discriminate when it came to men.

For his part, Knox was flattered and kind. He explained that he was a day late due to a family emergency, chatted for a few more minutes and accepted Summer's welcome to The Orchard Inn.

After he left to join the crew hired to begin restoration of the old train depot, Summer filled Harriet in on Madeline's condition. In return, Harriet relayed the messages that had come in during Summer's hour-long absence. Mentally she calculated the time it would take to launder the guest towels, dust the hardwood floors, pick a bouquet of lilacs for the dining room table and plan tomorrow's breakfast. In the back of her mind, she thought about Madeline's request.

She also wondered if Kyle had managed to catch his flight.

As if thoughts really did manifest into reality, the front door opened and Kyle walked in. Once again she had the distinct impression that nothing escaped his notice. It reminded her that she needed to stay on her toes with him.

"I left the inn ahead of you," she said. "And yet you arrived at the hospital before I did. How?"

He took his time removing his sunglasses, took his time replying. "I have a genetic predisposition to catch lights green and to bypass construction zones. I guess you could say I always get where I want to go."

Summer knew there was no logical reason to believe Kyle was referring in any way to sex, but *she* had a genetic predisposition to pay attention to innuendo. "I thought you had a plane to catch."

"Are you trying to get rid of me?" he asked.

"You evade a lot of questions," Summer said.

"We're alike that way," he countered.

Harriet looked up from the computer where she'd been checking out her new profile online and watched the exchange. Still sharp as a tack, she raised pencil-thin eyebrows at Summer as if concurring. Summer definitely needed to stay on her toes with this one.

"I didn't go to the airport because I decided that meeting my future sister-in-law was more important than catching a plane," Kyle said. "My brother's a lucky man. I don't think Madeline's midwife likes me, though. What's her secret?"

He was looking at Summer in waiting expectation, but it was Harriet who said, "Tayla doesn't like men. That's not a secret, though. I mean, she dates men on occasion, but she doesn't wholly trust the lot of you. And for your information, Summer doesn't reveal our secrets. She's a saint that way."

He met Summer's gaze. "You have a lot of fans."

"I have a lot of friends."

"Talya," he said thoughtfully. "It's the name of the Greek muse of comedy."

"You know the Muses?" Summer asked, thinking of the nine sister goddesses in Greek mythology presiding over song, poetry and the arts.

"As a writer, I'm well-acquainted with the muses." He leaned his elbows on the registration desk, the action bringing his face closer to Summer's. "How do *you* know them?"

"I studied mythology in college."

"What college?" he asked.

Summer didn't like answering questions about her past. Luckily Harriet liked to be the center of attention and saved Summer the trouble of trying to reply without revealing anything pertinent.

Harriet batted her fake eyelashes at Kyle and said, "Give me a second and I'll tell you what the name Kyle means."

Summer could have kissed her.

While Harriet clicked buttons on the computer, Kyle took out his credit card and slid it across the registration desk toward Summer. "I'm going to need that room for another night or two."

"You're not leaving for L.A.?" she asked.

He shook his head.

You have to be kidding me, she thought. But she feigned an apologetic smile and said, "I'm afraid all my rooms are taken." She could tell he didn't believe her.

"Here it is," Harriet said. "Kyle. It means handsome. They've got that right. I handed over the key to Room Seven ten minutes ago."

Kyle's green-eyed gaze was causing an atmospheric disturbance again. In the six-plus years Summer had lived here, she'd adjusted to an entirely new life, different in every way from the one she'd left behind. No more shopping trips to London or yachting on Sunday afternoons or going wherever she pleased whenever she pleased without having to worry about expenses. Now she worked for a living, and she worked hard.

When it came to friends, she'd taken a giant step up. She liked her new life. She loved her inn, and her friends and neighbors, and she enjoyed her niche in Orchard Hill.

Men were the only category she had trouble with. It wasn't that she didn't have opportunities to date. She went out often and truly enjoyed dinner and conversation. But she hadn't been wowed by any of them.

Until Kyle.

He was doing it again right now with just a look. "Have dinner with me," he said.

Peering up at Kyle through her trifocals, Harriet said, "I'd want to be home before seven. I hate to miss The Wheel."

Kyle seemed at a loss. Summer didn't try to hide her grin.

"Why don't you put Kyle in the attic apartment, dear?"

Just like that, Summer was the one at a loss, and Kyle's smile grew. He rounded the desk and planted a kiss on Harriet's lined, rouged cheek. "I'll take it. What time would you like me to pick you up for dinner? I promise to have you home in time for The Wheel."

Harriet fairly swooned as she named a time. "Would you like me to show him the attic?" she asked Summer.

"If you don't mind all those stairs," she said to her neighbor.

"It'll save me from having to get on the StairMaster."

With a wink at Kyle, Harriet added, "I like a tight butt."

There was a slight lifting of Kyle's right eyebrow as he looked down at the audacious, bodacious woman. He glanced at Summer and said, "So do I."

"How long will you be staying with us?" Summer asked, making a failed attempt to refrain from looking at Kyle's rear end as he sauntered toward the stairs.

"I'm not sure." He turned and caught her looking. "Oh. You need to know because of the room. I'll pay for an entire week. I'm doing Riley a favor, and I'm not sure how long it will take."

Summer was getting a bad feeling about this. "What kind of favor?" she asked.

"Madeline has doctor's orders to stay in bed, and Riley is going to wait on her hand and foot. They won't hear of postponing the wedding, so until Madeline's out of danger, I'm filling in for the groom. I'm not at all sure what that entails, exactly, since I've never been married. Do you?"

While Summer was shaking her head, Harriet put one hand on the newel post. In a stage whisper to Summer, she said, "If I'm not back in ten minutes, don't come looking for me."

Summer couldn't help smiling. "Don't do anything I wouldn't do."

Harriet's twitter preceded her up the stairs.

Kyle didn't immediately follow her. Sunlight spilled through the bay window, turning the air golden yellow. He stood in the middle of all that sunshine, feet slightly apart, hips narrow, the slight cleft in his chin more pronounced with the light behind him. He was tall and lean and wouldn't be very comfortable in the full-size bed in the attic apartment Madeline had recently vacated. He'd rented it sight unseen. That alone was cause for concern, for it suggested an agenda of some sort.

If that wasn't bad enough, he was looking at her again as if she were a puzzle he had every intention of solving. His name may have meant handsome, but he spelled trouble with a capital *T.*

"Are you coming?" Harriet called from the top of the first landing.

He glanced up the staircase and heaved a sigh. With his face turned slightly, his eyes hidden, Summer glimpsed a pallor not evident before. With his guard down, his fatigue was almost palpable.

She wondered if he'd been ill, or if there was something else at the root of his exhaustion. There was a weight in his step as he followed the purple-clad woman up the open staircase, the quiet thud of their footsteps overhead the only sounds Summer heard over the wild beating of her heart.

She faced the fact that Kyle Merrick wasn't going to be someone who'd once spent a night in her inn. He wasn't even going to be someone she'd once kissed. He would be staying in Orchard Hill for several days, and he would be sleeping right upstairs.

He'd agreed to fill in for the groom.

That was not what she'd wanted to hear. She could

feel the vein pulsing at her throat. That favor she'd wholeheartedly granted Madeline?

Summer had agreed to fill in for the bride.

bleep bleep bleep bleep bleep bleep
bleep-bleep bleep bleep bleep bleep
bleep bleep bleep bleep bleep bleep

Chapter Four

"**Y**ou missed your *bleeping* flight? Are you *bleep-bleep-bleeeeeeeeep?*"

Kyle held the phone slightly away from his ear to prevent permanent damage to his hearing. Grant Oberlin had a corner office on the top floor of a New York City high-rise with one of the most prestigious newspapers in the country. It had been one hell of a steep climb from the streets of south Boston where he'd grown up. Pushing sixty now, he hadn't lost his drive, the accent or the language.

"Where the *bleep* are you right now?"

Kyle had learned to mentally block out Grant's profanity. It was one of a handful of useful skills he'd gleaned from his father.

"On second thought," Grant said loudly. "I really

don't give a *bleep* where the *bleep* you are. Here's what you're going to do."

People in the business called Oberlin The Cowboy. He rolled his own cigarettes—he probably had one clamped between his lips right now—wore snakeskin cowboy boots and had a chip on his shoulder the size of Wyoming.

"Do you know how many *bleepity-bleep-bleep* strings I had to pull, how many favors I had to call in to get you this *bleeping* gig?"

The tirade continued. Kyle's mind wandered.

Harriet had opened the windows on either end of the attic before she'd gone. Kyle stood in the gentle cross breeze, his shirt unbuttoned, his feet bare.

The attic apartment was long and narrow. With its sloped ceilings and painted wood floors, it was the kind of space his interior decorator mother would have a name for. There was a bed and dresser on one end, a kitchenette and living room on the other, and a crooked chimney dividing the two halves. Harriet had said Madeline Sullivan had lived here after college. She must have taken all her personal touches with her, because the apartment was shades of gray and splashed with yellow. Like Summer.

"Get your bony *bleep* on the next plane, and I'll call Anderson and tell him you'll be in touch."

Oh. Grant was still talking.

The cagey newspaperman had given Kyle his first break fourteen years ago. Kyle had high regard for the man. There was a part of him screaming that Grant was right, that he was making a mistake or, as Grant put it, a mother-*bleeping* gargantuan *bleep*.

Kyle was too tired to care.

He took the verbal beating—he owed Grant that much—but he felt far removed from it. How long had it been, he wondered, since he'd felt anything? How long since his experiences had found their way through the top layers of his skin and moved him, touched him or just plain fazed him?

He was thirty-four years old and had become like one of those kids born without the sensor in their nerve endings that allowed them to feel pain. Without it, they didn't understand the concept of fire or sharp objects or broken bones. It was a dangerous way to live because, without pain, joy had a lot in common with a shot of Novocain.

"You haven't heard a *bleeping* word I've said, have you?"

Grant Oberlin was one of the few newsmen left willing to cut Kyle any slack. Maybe the only one. Kyle was numb to that, too.

He'd felt Summer's kiss, though. He conjured up the sensation from memory, her soft lips, her warm breath, her pliant body. He wasn't dead to everything.

"I heard you, Grant." His voice could have been coming from anybody, anywhere. "I'm on the scent of something here."

"Blonde, brunette or redhead?"

A year ago Kyle might have been able to rustle up a smile. "I have a hunch."

"Yeah, well, your *bleeping* hunches hold as much

water these days as a leaky bucket." How nice that Grant was moving from gutter slang to cliché.

"I'm not sure I care if I fix the bucket, Grant."

The blasé remark sparked a long litany of bleeps. "That's the trouble with you *bleeeep* kids who come into this profession already rich. You're not hungry enough."

Kyle had heard it before. That no longer fazed him, either. "I'll be in touch, Grant." He disconnected in the middle of the lecture.

Squeezing the phone in his fist, he almost hurled it against the wall. He yanked his shirt off, balled it up, and flung that instead. With that, the adrenaline leaked out of him like a stuck balloon.

Oberlin was wrong. Kyle *was* hungry. Hungry for something out of his reach, hungry for oblivion.

Flying day and night, night and day, living in airports and hotel rooms while hunting down people who didn't want to be found and sniffing out stories they didn't want to tell, sifting through lies and searching for a grain of truth, then writing an accurate account of the events only to have it slashed in half to make it fit in a column between a political cartoon and a story about a heroic cat that found its way home over the Rockies had grown wearisome.

Who wouldn't be tired?

Other than an occasional fluke, he'd lost the ability to sleep more than a few hours at a time. A friend of his who liked to play at psychiatry claimed his internal clock needed an adjustment. She said he needed to wake up and go to bed in the same time zone.

He needed to restore his reputation, too. And Kyle didn't see that happening.

He went to the window Harriet had opened. From here he had a bird's-eye view of the grounds and the river. In its day, rivers like this one had been an integral part of life in the Midwest. During the timber barons' heyday, logs were floated on the river to thriving sawmills downstream. Harriet said a riverboat used to travel from Lansing to Grand Haven and back every day, carrying commuters and travelers before the railroads were built and highways cut through the forests, around lakes, swamps and dunes.

He wondered if the river minded that it was no longer of use to anybody. Kyle knew the feeling.

Rumor was he'd sold out an informant. The proper terminology was that he was being investigated for revealing a source. He hadn't revealed anything, and he sure as hell hadn't taken money for it. But he couldn't prove it, and it had broken down the line of trust he'd worked so hard to build. And an investigative reporter without leads wasn't an investigative reporter for long.

He probably should care about that.

He had it from a good source that he was burned out. He wasn't burned out. And he wasn't experiencing writer's block, whatever the hell that was. He was just tired of fighting for meaningless front-page stories while the real news was given a two-inch spot after the obituaries.

Last night he'd slept more than he'd slept in weeks. It hadn't lasted. Already fatigue was engulfing him.

He turned his back on the view and glanced around

the room. Sloping ceilings, painted wood floors, a slip-covered sofa, mismatched lamps, and a bathroom too small to turn around in. He sank to the bed, because the accommodations didn't matter, either.

He laid back. And was asleep before he'd closed his eyes.

Summer's footsteps were quiet as she climbed the stairs to the third floor. At the top, she adjusted the stack of linens in her arms and finger combed her hair. She didn't really expect to see Kyle. After all, it had been three hours since Harriet had returned after showing him to his room. Although Summer hadn't heard the purling of the front door chimes or seen him leave through the kitchen where she'd been working this afternoon, it didn't mean he hadn't slipped out.

Just in case he was inside, she tapped lightly on the door. Placing her ear close, she listened. She didn't hear music, voices or the TV. There was only silence.

She hadn't spent much time in the third-floor apartment since Madeline had moved out two weeks ago. She'd given the place a thorough cleaning, but that was all she'd done. Since Kyle would need these towels before he could shower, and she wanted to make the bed up with fresh sheets, she knocked again. Her apartment off the kitchen and this one on the third floor were the only doors that required actual keys anymore. She had a spare key with her, but first she tried the knob. Surprisingly, it turned.

She'd have thought that somebody who'd lived in L.A.

and New York and half a dozen other bustling cities would have locked up behind him. Obviously not.

She would just run in, put the towels in the bathroom, freshen up the bed, then leave. She pushed the door open and instantly felt the gentle breeze.

The natural light slanting through the small windows on either end of the space left the center portion in shadow. Her hand was on the light switch when she saw Kyle lying on the bed across the room.

Shirtless and barefoot, he was clad in low-slung jeans. His face was turned toward her, his lashes casting deeper shadows on his cheeks. She saw no movement whatsoever, no fluttering of his eyes, not even a rise and fall of his chest. She thought about the pallor she'd glimpsed before he came upstairs and wondered—

She didn't like what she was thinking.

There were times in her life when she'd felt as if she were being steered toward a blind curve by an invisible hand pressed firmly against her back. Today she was being *pulled* toward it as if by an invisible cord.

As she crept steadily closer, she automatically categorized the space. She didn't see Kyle's duffel bag anywhere. His shirt lay half on, half off the chair beside the bed, his shoes lined up neatly beneath the window. The man was a study in contrasts. Somehow she'd expected that.

She hadn't expected him to be dead to the world. Cringing at her terminology, she saw no liquor bottles or sleeping pills on the nightstand, or anything else that might have explained his comatose appearance.

She leaned slightly over him. Now that she was only

a few feet away she could see his chest rise and fall shallowly. He was breathing. Thank heavens.

Okay, he was simply sound asleep. The voice of reason told her to stop looking at him, but my oh my oh my, she wasn't listening.

A man's chest really was his most attractive physical attribute. No man wanted to hear that, but it was true. Kyle's chest was muscled, the skin taut and tan and darkened with a sparse mat of fine, brown hair. His ribs showed, suggesting a lanky, wiry build. His waist was lean, his abs tidily halved by a narrow line of hair that disappeared beneath the closure of his CK's.

She had no idea how he kept in shape, but he was every woman's fantasy and had a broad appeal that could have been an advertisement for anything from blue jeans to sports cars to European vacations. His legs were long and lean, too. Shame on her for allowing her eyes to linger at his fly.

Summer took a step away and let her gaze glide back along a safer path—waist, abs, ribs, chest, shoulders. His jaw was darkened with whisker stubble. His mouth was closed.

And his eyes were slightly open.

She froze like a deer trapped in the glare of headlights. He was looking at her.

Or was he?

She looked closer and realized she was wrong. His eyes were open a slit but his pupils weren't focused. He was still sound asleep.

And she was getting out of here before he woke up and caught her watching him or worse. But what could

be worse? He could accuse her of liking what she saw.
She couldn't have refuted it, for she evaded the truth
when necessary, but she didn't lie.

She scurried to the door on tiptoe, leaving the towels
and sheets on the table where Kyle had left his keys.
She backed out the door, her gaze on his prone form,
an image that was going to be nearly impossible to get
out of her mind.

Kyle was aware of two things when he wandered
downstairs. His brain was fuzzy despite his quick
shower, and he was starving.

He wasn't wearing a watch, and he'd left his cell
phone charging next to the stack of towels he'd discovered by his door, so he couldn't be certain of the time.
He'd missed lunch. From the look of the activity of other
guests at the inn, their work was over for the day.

Two men in blue jeans and work boots stood on the
portico, their voices carrying through the screen door.
Three others sat around what appeared to be an old
game table in the front room off the foyer. A kid who
didn't look old enough to shave was eating fast food in
the dining room. The aroma of greasy fries had Kyle's
stomach growling all the way to the kitchen.

He hadn't known what he was looking for until he
saw her. *Summer.*

She stood at the counter, her back to him. She was
whipping up something with a wire whisk, her actions
slowing each time she glanced at the recipe book open
in front of her. Her light brown hair swished between

her shoulder blades and her hips swayed to and fro with every repetition of that metal whisk.

She must have had ultra-sensitive hearing, for she glanced over her shoulder. Stilling momentarily, she said, "You're awake."

He sauntered the rest of the way into the room, letting the door swing closed behind him. "Jet lag's a b— a bear."

"I see you found the bath towels," she said, resuming whatever it was she was doing.

So, she'd noticed his damp hair. Obviously he wasn't the only observant type in the room. He stopped at the kitchen table and said, "Until I spotted the towels, I thought I'd imagined seeing you in my room."

She stopped stirring. "You saw me?"

"I've got to tell you, it was a relief finding evidence that you'd been there. Chronic insomnia and an insatiable hunger are bad enough. Hallucinations would have been a lot tougher to ignore."

She smiled at his dry wit. He found he liked that, too.

"I thought you were dead," she said, as she faced him. "Seriously, I've never seen anybody sleep so soundly. If you saw me deliver your towels, why didn't you say something?"

"Like I said, I thought I was dreaming. I'd be happy to tell you about the rest of the dream."

She rested her back against the counter, folded her arms and tilted her head slightly. He half expected a mild admonishment. He felt a sexual stirring again. Oh, he definitely wasn't numb to everything.

"Harriet is the one who enjoys dirty stories," she said quietly.

Did she say Harriet?

There was a nagging buzzing in the back of his mind. He looked from Summer's hazel eyes to the clock on the stove. It was after seven.

Harriet.

He'd stood her up. Muttering Grant Oberlin's favorite word under his breath, Kyle headed for the door.

"Take these," Summer told him. She handed him a vase filled with fragrant lilacs. "Purple is Harriet's favorite color."

It was dark outside when Kyle parked at the curb in front of Madeline's house on Floral Avenue later that night. He recognized Riley's silver car in the driveway and also Summer's blue sedan. Two other vehicles were there, too. It might have explained why every light in the house was on.

He climbed out of his Jeep, only to hesitate. Madeline's doctor had prescribed bed rest, so it was unlikely there was a wild party going on, and yet for a few seconds he wondered if he should go in. Riley would have called Kyle a choice brotherly name if he knew Kyle was so much as considering the possibility that he was intruding.

Riley, Braden and Kyle had been raised by three very different mothers in three separate households. The boys had all wanted the same thing from their father: his attention, some fatherly advice and a good example. Brock Merrick hadn't had it in him. He'd shared his immense wealth, and he'd loved his sons; he'd loved their mothers, too. The problem was, he'd loved a lot of women. By the time the boys were adults, they'd learned to accept his flaw. Ultimately, since they couldn't get what they'd needed from him, they'd gotten it from each other. They'd also gotten black eyes and bruised egos, but that was part of growing up with brothers.

They'd vowed to be there for one another no matter what, no questions asked, and while they'd all been adults for a while now and didn't see each other as often as they wanted to, being there for one another would never change. Feeling back in his game, Kyle walked to his brother's door.

Riley answered Kyle's knock and threw the door wide. He motioned him in as if Kyle were a lifeboat and Riley was swimming in shark-infested water. "I'm glad you're here."

"Is something wrong?" Kyle asked.

This morning only Riley and his dog, Gulliver, had been home. Tonight, Kyle heard voices, several of them. All female.

"No," Riley said. "On the other hand." He paused again. "No, come on back."

Kyle wondered, was there something wrong or not?

Just then a chorus of laughter carried through the house. One was throaty, one breathy, one a giggle. Again, all were feminine. Maybe there was a party going on after all.

Gulliver looked expectantly at Riley then waited for his master to nod before leading the way. The brown dog and Riley took the same route through Madeline's house they'd taken this morning. They led Kyle past a narrow staircase in the living room then through a brightly lighted dining room and into the kitchen. From there they entered an arched hallway where Kyle saw a door that had been closed earlier.

They stopped outside a small bedroom with old-fashioned floral wallpaper and period furnishings. There was a mahogany desk and dresser on the far wall. On an adjacent wall was an antique four-poster bed. And on that four-poster were four women.

Kyle recognized Summer. She sat on the side closest to the door, her back to him, her body blocking the faces of two others. Kyle assumed the slight woman lying down was Madeline. He had no idea who the other two lined up against the headboard were. One had a note-book open on her lap, the other was gesturing wildly with her hands. Whatever she said caused laughter to erupt again.

Kyle and Riley shared a look, and Kyle quietly said, "This kind of thing would never happen between men."

Riley's sudden chuckle drew four sets of eyes. It occurred to Kyle that laughter looked good on Summer. Her cheeks were flushed, the curve of her lips enticing a second look. Rimmed by dark lashes, her eyes crinkled slightly at the corners. She was smiling, genuinely happy.

There was an innate elegance in the way she placed her teacup on its gilded saucer and set it on the night-stand before introducing him to her friends. Chelsea

Reynolds was the curvy brunette, Abby Fitzpatrick the wispy-haired blonde.

"It's nice to meet you," he said to each in turn.

"How did it go?" Summer asked him.

"Better than I expected."

"Did she forgive you?"

"Who?" the petite blonde asked.

The brunette shushed her with a nudge.

"She made me work for it," he said, his gaze steady on Summer. He and Summer were the only ones who knew they were referring to Harriet Ferris, and neither of them chose to explain to the others. "But eventually she warmed up," Kyle said. "The flowers were a big help."

"I'm glad." She was looking at him as if she meant it.

Kyle wondered if anybody else in the room noticed that he couldn't seem to take his eyes off her. He was interested. He was intrigued. And he hadn't been either of those things in a while.

"Am I interrupting something?" he asked her.

Summer shook her head. "Chelsea is Madeline's wedding planner. She's been prioritizing the most pressing details for the coming week."

The blonde, Abby, said, "Summer's going to be filling in for Madeline."

"Is that right?" He smiled at Abby, but his gaze ultimately went to Summer again, for this was the first he'd heard that.

The weather had been unseasonably warm and humid today. It brought out the beast in a lot of people. As far as Kyle was concerned, the conditions were perfect for peeling off layers of clothing, for gliding a zipper down a slender back, for lowering the straps of a certain someone's bra and for taking his time removing it.

That was a good place to halt his wayward thoughts. "If you have plans to make," he said, looking directly at Summer, "I won't keep you from them." Even he could hear the huskiness in his voice. "I just stopped over to talk to Riley." Kyle nodded at all four women. He smiled last at Summer.

He'd been accused of being vain a time or two. When he happened to look over his shoulder as he was leaving and caught four women looking at him, he knew why he'd never apologized for it.

From the doorway, he directed a question to the official wedding planner of the group. "I'm curious about something. What does a fill-in bride do?"

Chelsea held up the fingers of her right hand and began listing off responsibilities. "She hosts a bridal shower, samples wedding cake, chooses the menu, wears pink, the bride's favorite color." That was spoken with a shudder. "She helps the bride select the music, meets with the photographer and basically does whatever needs to be done, even if it means keeping the appointment with the seamstress for the final dress fitting, since, luckily, Summer and Madeline are the same size."

Summer was shaking her head. "Trying on someone else's wedding gown is bad luck."

Obviously, this was an ongoing debate.

"Now you sound like Madeline," the petite blonde

said. "Usually she's the one with all the uncanny intuitions and crazy premonitions."

"I'm right here," Madeline said. "And I can hear everything you're saying, Abs."

Kyle couldn't help smiling. He would have enjoyed continuing along that vein, but he said, "And what does the fill-in groom do?" He'd already spoken to Riley about this, but his brother's answer had been sketchy at best.

He doubted there were many women who could pull off appearing businesslike while sharing a bed with three other women, but Chelsea made an admirable attempt as she held up the fingers of her right hand again and prepared to count the ways Kyle could help this week. In the end, all her fingers remained straight.

"I suppose the groom's responsibility during the week prior to the wedding is to support the bride."

His gaze returned to Summer's. In this instance he would be supporting the *fill-in* bride. "I can do that," he said.

Her hair had fallen across her cheek. He would have liked to brush it away. As long as he was touching her, he would glide his finger to her chin, his thumb smoothing over her lower lip. He'd let his hand trail down her neck, stopping at the little vein pulsing in the delicate hollow.

Kyle felt the way he had earlier. Alive and aware. Especially aware. If he and Summer had been alone, there was no telling what he might have done. Instead, he reined in his hormones and smiled all around.

"It was nice meeting both of you," he said to Abby

and Chelsea. "Take care of yourself, Madeline." At last he spoke to the woman he couldn't seem to stop looking at. "Summer. I guess I'll see you at the inn."

Summer swore the temperature lowered ten degrees the minute the men left the room. She heard three collective sighs from the other women on the bed. Pleased to discover that her hand was still steady, she took a sip of tea.

"Holy moly," Madeline declared.

"What was that?" Abby whispered.

"That," Chelsea declared, "was one amazing example of pure masculine appeal."

"That," Summer qualified, "was Kyle Merrick being supportive."

Madeline was looking at Summer, one eyebrow raised. With a point of her finger, Summer said, "Don't start."

Madeline grinned knowingly. And Summer thought it was going to be a long week.

"He wants you," Chelsea said matter-of-factly.

"Film at eleven," Abby piped in.

Arguing that they were wrong would have been futile, and Summer had a feeling she needed to save her strength. For a few moments, she'd almost forgotten that Kyle was in a profession she mistrusted. For those few blessed minutes, he'd simply been someone who slept too soundly and lost track of time and made her lose track of it, too. He was someone who took a bouquet of lilacs to a kind old lady, someone who brought out yearnings Summer hadn't expected to feel. It was too late to chide herself, for Chelsea was right.

He wanted her.

He hadn't tried to hide it. She hadn't expected that any more than she'd expected him to show up here tonight or arrive last night during that thunderstorm. But he had, and he wasn't leaving anytime soon.

Being wanted by a man like him was heady. It was tempting, and normally Summer didn't tempt easily. What she didn't know was what she was going to do about it.

Chapter Five

Kyle tossed the crime novel he'd been reading onto the bed. It landed facedown on the rumpled pillow beside him. Picking up the remote again, he aimed it at the small television on the nearby wall, adjusted his pillows and tried to get comfortable. He'd already caught the beginning of a comedian's act, a portion of the race Braden had qualified for in Europe, and the end of a black and white war movie. He'd watched an infomercial selling kitchen knives, a lot of garbage, and a piece about the disappearing rain forests in South America.

He stayed away from the news.

Powering off the television, he sat up on the edge of the bed. By the light of a small lamp in the alcove that distinguished the bedroom from the living room, he padded quietly to the window. He stood in the shadows looking up at the sky. There, in the west, was Pleiades.

According to an ancient Greek legend, the bright cluster of stars represented seven sisters who'd been openly pursued by a relentless hunter named Orion. Zeus, the ruler of the gods, took pity on the beautiful maidens and changed them into doves before setting them free into the heavens.

Those ancient stargazers sure knew how to tell a story. They must have spent a lot of time studying the night sky. Kyle wondered if they'd been insomniacs, too.

The inn settled around him. Somewhere a car downshifted. The air outside his window was still, the night so quiet he could hear the river flowing over the rocks in the distance. The dark windows of the neighboring houses reflected the crescent moon. Old post lamps lined the driveway and lit the inn's front lawn. The only illumination in the backyard was a square patch of yellow stretching onto the grass close to the inn. He couldn't see the origin of that light but he could tell from the angle that it was coming from the first floor.

He wasn't the only one awake at this hour.

Summer swirled the pale wine in her glass. After enjoying a generous sip, she returned to the stove where she stirred hot cream into a bowl containing beaten egg yolks and sugar. Humming with the radio, she then poured the mixture into the saucepan, adjusted the flame and began to slowly stir.

She loved cooking at night, loved the rhythm, the aroma and the steam. The process of measuring and mixing, folding and stirring was soothing. It cleared her mind, which helped her contemplate solutions to problems.

Take Kyle Merrick for instance. He was an investigative reporter. Of all the legitimate professions in the world, his had the potential to be the most damaging to the new life she'd built. That made this attraction anything but safe.

No wonder she'd been genuinely *relieved* when she'd learned he wouldn't be attending Madeline's wedding. Now he was staying in The Orchard Inn. What were the chances of that happening? she wondered.

She'd fairly melted in his arms when he'd kissed her in this very kitchen. She couldn't very well pretend indifference now without raising his suspicions. Besides, she wasn't that good an actress.

As she stirred the mixture in the saucepan, it occurred to her that having Kyle under her roof might not be so terrible after all. She needed to set some boundaries, for sure, but having him in close proximity meant she could keep an eye on him.

She took another sip from her fluted glass and turned down the flame under the front burner. The stove was forty-five years old and was often cantankerous, but tonight it was cooperating beautifully. Her crème brulee would be a masterpiece. She stirred and hummed, and hummed and stirred, her mind on the sweet concoction and the little oasis of light she'd created in the otherwise dark inn.

She liked nearly everything about her life as an innkeeper. Keeping this place running smoothly and in the black brought her a sense of accomplishment she hadn't known until she'd taken on the responsibility shortly after coming to Orchard Hill. She enjoyed serving breakfast and especially liked meeting new people and hearing all about their lives and dreams. She'd come to appreciate the steady progression and the one hundred and one tasks from check-in to checkout. She didn't mind the daily punctiliousness of freshening rooms and shopping and seeing to her guests' needs. The daylight hours belonged to them.

The night was hers.

Tonight the air was unseasonably warm. Thanks to the apple trees in the nearby orchards resplendent with blossoms, it was also wonderfully fragrant.

Turning off the flame beneath the thickened concoction, she sniffed the rising steam. With a moan, she closed her eyes.

When she opened them, she was no longer alone.

Kyle stood in the doorway where the light was faint, one hand on his hip and an easy smile playing at the corners of his mouth. "Am I interrupting?"

Always with that lilting sensuality. Deciding there was no time like the present to implement the boundaries she needed to set, she gave him a friendly smile and said, "You're welcome to come in, on one condition." She scooped up a spoonful of the hot mixture and gently blew on it. "Try this."

He sauntered to the stove wearing loafers, faded jeans and a T-shirt with wording in French. Bringing his nose close to her spoon, he took a trial whiff.

There was a certain level of trust involved as he

touched his lips to the still warm dessert. It was his turn to moan.

She reached for another spoon and sampled some, too. "That's not half-bad, is it?"

"Half-bad? Are you kidding? It's magnificent." Kyle moved slightly to make room for Summer as she went to the sink and washed her hands. She was wearing a white tank top and those knit pants that looked so damn good on women. Hers rode low on her hips and were held up by a string tied in a loose bow.

"Do you always cook when everyone else is sleeping?" he asked.

"It's when I enjoy it the most, and when I have the most time for it. The first strawberries of the season are ripe," she said as she dried her hands on a yellow towel. "I thought I'd spoon the crème brulee over them and offer a bowlful to my guests with breakfast which, by the way, is served every weekday between seven and nine."

Her movements were fluid, her voice quiet, as if in reverence to the night. She must have seen him looking hungrily at the crème brulee, for she took a bowl from the cupboard, filled it, added a clean spoon and handed it to him.

The bottom of the dish was warm in his palm, the aroma wafting upwards so sweet smelling his mouth watered. He didn't dig right in, though.

"Is something wrong?" she asked.

"Aren't you going to have any?"

It didn't take her long to make up her mind. Soon

they were leaning against opposite cupboards, ankles crossed, bowls in one hand, spoons in the other.

"So," she said between bites, "are you going to see Harriet again?"

Kyle didn't know whether to laugh or scoff. Everything about Summer Matthews was a contrast. The way she'd ladled her concoction into bowls and daintily ate it was refined. Her reference to his date bordered on brazen. Earlier she'd been sipping tea. Now her wine glass was empty. She was as regal as royalty, and yet she seemed to run this inn single-handedly. It couldn't be easy to keep up with the repairs of a building this old—floors pitched, doors didn't close, pipes rattled. And yet every item in the house had so obviously been *chosen*. The retro range and state-of-the-art refrigerator and the scratched oak table and cane-bottom chairs sitting tidily on an aubusson rug didn't scream good taste. They whispered it.

"I think I met Harriet's secret tonight," he said, scraping the bottom of his bowl.

Summer's eyebrows rose slightly. "Her secret?"

"Walter."

"You met Walter?"

"He joined us for dinner." Kyle emptied his bowl only to have it miraculously refilled. It happened again before he'd finished telling Summer about the evening.

Walter Ferris was a large man with beefy hands, thick gray hair and bushy eyebrows. He'd probably been a handsome devil once. In his late seventies, he was straightforward and astute. He hadn't been able to take his eyes off Harriet all night. Harriet had given Kyle plenty of attention, but he'd caught her eyes going soft on Walter a time or two when she'd thought Kyle wasn't looking.

They had history, no doubt about it. And since they had the same last name, and they didn't act like kissing cousins, Kyle wondered what their connection really was.

He didn't normally give relationships more than a passing thought. It had been a long time since he'd been in one that lasted more than a month or two. He'd *never* stood in a woman's kitchen eating warm crème brulee at three in the morning. Maybe there was something to the adage that the way to a man's heart was through his stomach, although Kyle preferred other more evocative ways.

"Do I have crème brulee on my chin?" she asked.

He shook his head but didn't apologize for staring. "What were we talking about?"

She seemed to have forgotten, too. It made them both smile.

"Walter," they said in unison.

Walter Ferris had a story for every occasion but, other than a vague recollection of Summer mentioning a mother and sister who'd died before she'd moved to Orchard Hill, neither he nor Harriet seemed to know a lot about her past.

"I'm a little surprised Walter joined you tonight," Summer said. "They usually have dinner together on Tuesdays and Fridays."

Kyle stared at her, his spoon poised between his

mouth and bowl. "Are you saying Harriet and Walter have regular dinner date nights?"

She'd spooned another bite into her mouth and therefore couldn't answer. He wondered if evading questions was intentional or automatic.

"Are they married then? Ah," he said, finally understanding the dynamics. "They're divorced. If I were to harbor a guess, I'd say Walter wants her back. Men are easy to read that way."

"I don't like to talk about people behind their backs," she said.

"If you'd rather we can talk about us."

Summer used the ruse of carrying Kyle's empty bowl to the sink to buy her a little time. It also gave her a little much-needed space.

By the time she'd rinsed the bowls, he was leaning against the countertop in the inn's main kitchen again, his ankles crossed, arms folded. If she'd stopped there, she would have believed he was completely at ease. But it only required one look at his lean face, his lips firmly together, his green eyes hooded, and she knew the ease was secondary. He was a man who took nothing for granted, a man who didn't rush or gloss over details. He was the kind of man who would take his time pleasuring a woman.

"There is no *us*," she said. What was wrong with her voice?

"Not yet, you mean."

It was the perfect opening for her to say, "You and I don't know each other, Kyle. You're just passing through

Orchard Hill, but I live in this town. My livelihood is hinged on my reputation."

He uncrossed his ankles and straightened, leading her to assume he was going to take the rejection with a grain of salt and go back upstairs. Instead he joined her in front of the sink.

"Sunrise or sunset?" he asked.

"What?"

"Sunrise or sunset?" he repeated.

She'd turned the radio down when he'd first joined her in the kitchen. Now the low hum barely covered the quiet. "What are you talking about?" she asked.

"I'm getting to know you. I think the modern terminology refers to this stage as the date interview. You're right, that's an easy one. You are sunset all the way. It's your turn. Go ahead, ask me anything."

She started the faucet and squirted dish soap into the stream. "This isn't a date," she reminded him sternly, but she couldn't help thinking he was right about her and sunsets.

What could it hurt, she thought, to participate in a little harmless middle of the night conversation? After considering possible safe topics, she said, "Bourbon or Merlot?"

"Bourbon, hands down."

She was surprised. She'd have pegged him as the kind of man who had an extensive wine collection.

"Hard rock or Rap?" he asked when it was his turn. "First, what are you doing?" He pointed at the sink she was filling with sudsy water.

"The dishwasher's broken, and there won't be money

in the budget to have it repaired until July," she explained. "Hard rock and Rap are both okay on occasion, but my favorite musician of all time is Leonard Cohen."

As two iridescent bubbles floated on the rising steam, he said, "So you're a romantic at heart."

Had he moved closer? Or had she? Putting a little space between them again, she scoured a saucepan.

Kyle said, "I'd offer to fix your dishwasher, but I'm afraid my brother Braden is the mechanical genius in the family. I'm good with my hands in other ways."

"I'm sure you'll be very happy with yourself."

His laugh was a deep rumble, the kind that invited everyone to smile along. They were standing close again, her shoulder nearly touching his arm. This time he was the one who moved slightly. Picking up a towel, he began to dry. "I believe it's your turn."

Hmm, she thought as she washed measuring cups and spoons. "Baseball or football?"

"Football, but I like races the best. European Auto Racing is my favorite, probably because my youngest brother is trying to break records and hopefully not his neck. Chicken or fish?"

"I'm more of a pasta girl. Dogs or cats?"

"Dogs," he said. "Friends or family?"

Rinsing her wine glass and carefully handing it to him by the stem, she said, "I don't have much family."

"Then it wasn't a family connection that brought you to Orchard Hill?"

Keeping her wits about her, she said, "Madeline likes to say Orchard Hill found me. The elderly couple that used to own The Orchard Inn had been looking for someone to take it over. I applied, and the rest is history."

"So you work for this old couple?" he asked.

"I bought the inn from them with the money my grandmother left me. She'd been very ill and died right after I moved here." Summer's grandmother had been the only one who knew where she went, and the estate attorney had promised to keep her location confidential.

"The grandmother you and your sister spent summers with on Mackinaw Island?" he asked.

She supposed she shouldn't have been surprised he'd been listening when she'd mentioned that. Keeping her eyes on the dish she was washing, she said, "I wasn't kidding when I told you I don't have much family."

"If you'd like, you can borrow some of mine. Other than Riley and Braden, most of our relatives are female. One mother, two stepmothers and too many grandmothers, aunts and family pets to count. Action-adventure or horror?"

She laughed at the awkward segue. "I live alone in a hundred-and-twenty-year-old inn. Definitely not horror." It was her turn to ask a question. She took her time deciding which one. "Crime dramas or reality TV?"

"Could I get another choice here?"

"You don't watch much television?" she asked.

He made a sound universal to men through his pursed lips. "Three hundred channels and there's still nothing on half the time."

She looked up at him and smiled, for she'd often thought the same thing.

"See what I mean?" he said, his voice a low croon befitting the dark night. "We have a lot in common. We're practically soul mates."

She wished she could blame the warm swirl in the pit of her stomach on the lateness of the hour or the wine. "Out of all these questions," she said, "we've found only one thing we have in common. I don't believe in soul mates."

His gaze went from her eyes, to her lips, to the base of her neck where a little vein was pulsing. He folded the towel over the edge of the sink and got caught looking at her lips again. He didn't pretend he didn't want to kiss her. And yet he waited. A man who had enough self-confidence to want a woman to be sure wasn't an easy man to resist.

A gentle breeze stirred the air. Somewhere a night bird warbled. Moments later an answering call sounded from across the river. Summer didn't recognize the birdsong, but she understood the language of courtship. It seemed to her that birds had a straightforward approach to life. They built a nest in the spring, raised a brood and, as if guided by some magical internal alarm clock, they gathered in flocks and flew south to a tropical paradise for the winter, only to return and start all over again in the spring.

Summer had started over once. She never wanted to do that again, which brought her right back to where she and Kyle had started. Whatever this was, be it a date interview or simply a pleasant interlude, it was ending. It had to.

Taking a deliberate step back, she said, "Good night, Kyle."

He handled the mild rejection with a degree of watchfulness and his usual charm. She wasn't expecting the light kiss. Little more than a brush of air, it was over by the time she'd closed her eyes. The dreamy intimacy lingered as he walked to the door.

"Thank you for the midnight snack," he said quietly, "and for having a sunset personality."

She smiled. And he was gone.

It was a few minutes before Summer's heart settled into its normal rhythm. Occasionally Madeline used to join her in the kitchen late at night. Kyle was the only *man* who ever had. Strangely, his presence hadn't been an intrusion. Without even trying, he'd made her feel understood. Kyle Merrick would make a good friend.

He would have been a good lover, too. Of that, she had no doubt. All things considered, his middle of the night visit had gone well. He seemed to have accepted the limits she'd set. It was a relief, and yet, with every swish of the drawstring at her waist and every rustle of the fabric at her midriff, she was reminded of what she was missing.

She stuck her hands on her hips and huffed. She supposed there was always the next best thing.

On the counter sat the uncorked bottle of wine and the bowl containing the remaining crème brulee. She pushed the wine out of the way and reached for a spoon.

Friday morning dawned cloudy and gray. The temperature had dropped overnight and the barometric pressure had been on the rise ever since. Spring had returned to Orchard Hill.

Seven of Summer's eight guests had shuffled to the breakfast table groggy or grumpy or both, adversely affected by the atmospheric change. Kyle was the last to amble downstairs. Looking surprisingly rested and amiable, he took a seat at the long dining room table as she was clearing away the place settings of five men who'd already left for their day's work restoring the train depot.

"Good morning," she said, as she did to each guest every day.

"Morning," he answered. "Beautiful day, isn't it?"

The last two remaining carpenters looked askance at him. When thunder rumbled an exclamation point disguised as weather, Kyle had the grace to counter his sunny outlook with, "Easy for me to say. I'm not being forced to work in it today."

With a few grumbles, he was forgiven.

"Coffee and juice are on the sideboard," she said. "I'll be right back with your breakfast."

Kyle was alone at the table with his coffee when she returned with his plate of crisp bacon, whole wheat toast and a stack of piping hot pancakes. In a separate bowl was a generous serving of fresh strawberries sans crème brulee.

"Have you already had breakfast?" he asked.

She thought about the slice of toast she'd eaten two hours ago while the bacon was frying and answered simply, "Yes."

"A cup of coffee, then?" he asked.

Summer had hit the snooze button once, and then she'd hit the floor running. She hadn't slept well the previous night, and, after only three hours last night, sleep deprivation was catching up with her. Caffeine sounded wonderful. In fact, she could have used a direct IV line of the stuff. She went to the sideboard and poured herself a piping hot cup.

It wasn't unusual for her to have a cup of coffee with a guest. Her boarders all happened to be men this month, but that wasn't always the case. Sometimes families stayed here. Throughout the year, groups of women came for girlfriends' weekends of wine tasting and shopping and marathon chick flick rentals. Summer's mainstay came from sales reps and other men and women employed by companies with projects too far away for a reasonable commute.

She sipped her coffee while Kyle dug into his breakfast. They talked about everyday things. He told her about a book he was reading, and she relayed a funny story from a former guest. Out of the blue, he asked her if she'd ever been married.

She looked him in the eye and with complete honesty said, "No, have you?"

He offered her a pancake before he drizzled the stack with syrup. She took it and daintily ate it with her fingers while he explained why he'd never married.

She was laughing by the time he summed it up. "Women are complicated."

"And men aren't?" she asked.

Cutting into his stack of pancakes, he said, "I'd be

happy to explain the differences to you, but I have to warn you, it's not a topic for sissies."

Somehow she believed he was only half joking. In a like manner, she said, "I'm fairly certain I can handle it."

He seemed to be enjoying the opportunity to share his expertise. The man obviously had a playful side to go with his voracious appetite. The pallor she'd glimpsed yesterday was less noticeable this morning. His eyes crinkled at the corners, as green and changeable as the weather. He hadn't bothered to shave. The stubble on his jaw was a shade darker than his hair. The collar of his shirt was open at his throat, the green broadcloth a color and style that would fit in anywhere.

"Basically there are five classifications of men," he began as he spread jelly on his toast. "The butt heads are by and large the worst. Normally I would refer to them as something more crass, but I'm going to try to do this delicately, so we'll stick with butt heads. These are the guys who make promises they have no intention of keeping. They're hard and heartless. These are the liars, stealers, cheaters, politicians, CEOs, anybody with no conscience. They give all men a bad name."

She was listening, for she'd once known a few of those. Intimately.

"Next are the sorry-asses. Forgive me but there's no delicate way to describe this category. They're the drunks, the guys who mean well but are too lazy to bring home a paycheck, get their own beer or mow the lawn. You know, your basic losers."

She couldn't help smiling again.

"Third is the—let's call the third category the dumb-bells. If sorry-asses are your basic losers, dumbbells are your basic users. This is the guy who doesn't have any money with him on Pizza Friday, who has to be shown repeatedly how to use the business system at work but can navigate every search engine for his personal use on company time. He's more obnoxious than harmful."

She made an agreeable sound, which earned her an appreciative masculine grin that went straight to her head.

"The last two categories are the smart alecks and the wise guys. At first glance you might think they're one and the same. They're both on the mouthy side, but smart alecks are irritating and wise guys are charming and entertaining." He took a big bite of his pancakes and smiled smugly, as if his work here was done.

"You've certainly cleared that up," she said over the rim of her coffee cup. "Tell me this. Why do women put up with any of you?"

Those green eyes of his spoke a full five seconds before he said, "Because some of us are irresistible."

"You don't say."

They fell into a companionable silence. She finished the plain pancake and sipped her coffee, and he made a good-sized dent in his breakfast.

Thunder rumbled overhead. Kyle felt an answering vibration that was more like the pulsing beat of a distant drum than weather. It started deep inside, radiating outward. This was desire, the kind that burned slow and got hotter. There was only one way to appease it, and she was sitting across the table from him.

Summer's dress was the color of pecans today. When was the last time he'd met a woman who wore a dress every day? He wasn't referring to buttoned-up suits with pencil-thin skirts and stiletto heels with toes so pointy they could draw blood. Summer wasn't out for blood. Was that why she drew him?

No. There was something far more elemental at work here.

Her dress was sleeveless, and the neckline covered all but the inside edges of her collarbones. It wasn't formfitting or tight and had no business looking sexy. He wanted to push his plate away and reach for her, but burning off this hunger with her wasn't going to be that simple.

Luckily Kyle was a patient man.

When his plate was empty, she came around to his side of the table and took it. Pausing at the kitchen door, she glanced back at him and said, "Which type are you?"

He wiped his mouth on his napkin and stood. "If you have to ask, I'm doing something wrong." With that he sauntered out the front door.

In the kitchen, Summer turned on the hot water and squirted in dish soap. As suds expanded over the dishes in the bottom, she placed one finger over that little indentation at the base of her neck. Feeling the pulse fluttering there, she thought, a wise guy, definitely.

Since there were no parking spaces in front of Rose's Flower Shoppe, Summer parked in front of Knight's Bakery and Confectionary Shoppe a block away. The steady pitter-patter of raindrops on her umbrella muffled the click of her heels as she started toward Rose's, but it didn't dampen her mood. Betty Ryan smiled from the window of her daughter and son-in-law's bakery when she saw Summer walking by. Looking up from the newspaper he was reading in his barber chair, Bud Barkley wiggled his fingers at Summer. She couldn't help returning his classic wave.

She hurried past two clothing stores that had survived the ongoing feud between their owners *and* the recession. The big chains had drained the life out of the old drugstore on the corner. Now the building was home to Izzy's Ice Cream Parlor. Summer loved that she knew the stories and the struggles of the courageous, tenacious people who called Orchard Hill home. Being accepted by them was an honor and a gift.

As if on cue, her phone jangled in her purse. Sliding it open, she began talking the moment she put it to her ear. "I'm on my way, Chelsea. How's Madeline this morning?"

"She's going stir-crazy and Riley's hovering." Chelsea's voice in her ear was clear and concise. "I don't know who I feel sorrier for. Let me know what Josie says about Madeline's bouquet, okay? I know you can't be away from the inn more than absolutely necessary, so somebody from Knight's Bakery is bringing four samples of wedding cake to the inn later."

Flowers. Check.

Wedding cake. Check.

There was something Summer was forgetting, but Chelsea was on a mission, and, when that happened, there was no stopping her. "Reverend Brown has agreed to go to Madeline's house after services on Sunday to talk to her and Riley about the ceremony and vows. That'll take us to the final five-day countdown. Can you believe it?"

Summer thought it *was* amazing how fast the wedding was approaching, but she didn't have an opportunity to make more than an agreeable murmur before Chelsea had to take another call. Outwardly Chelsea Reynolds was the most organized young woman on the planet. But underneath her buttoned-up shirts and practical manner smoldered a dreamer. Only those closest to her knew the reason she kept it hidden.

The world was feeling like a good place as Summer dropped her phone back into her shoulder bag and walked into Rose's Flower Shoppe. As always, the scents of carnations and roses met her at the door.

"I'll be right with you." Josie Rose's muffled voice sounded as if she was speaking into the cooler. Eight months pregnant with her third child, she entered the room with one hand at the small of her back and the other on her basketball-size belly. "There you are, Summer. Someone was here a little while ago asking about you. A man," she said in a stage whisper.

For the span of one heartbeat, Summer's only thought was, *they've found me.* She waited, unmoving.

"Can you say tall, dark and handsome?" Josie asked, oblivious to Summer's inner turmoil.

Oh. Okay. Summer could breathe again, because that description ruled out Drake and her father.

When she'd first moved to Orchard Hill and shortened

her name and bought her inn, she'd often caught herself looking over her shoulder. There had been times when she'd been certain someone was following her. She wasn't afraid, physically, of her former fiancé or her father. It was the havoc they could wreak and the media circus they were capable of creating that she so dreaded. Her father had connections to people in high places. She'd seen him in action with her own two eyes and knew he had the ability and the capability to ruin people for pleasure or personal gain.

Nothing had ever materialized out of those certainties that she was being followed. Eventually her paranoia subsided. She relaxed and began to enjoy the life she was painstakingly building, but old habits died hard, and this morning dread had reared.

"He had the greenest eyes I've ever seen on a man," Josie continued.

Summer knew only one man who fit that description. "I think you're referring to Riley's brother Kyle. He's staying at the inn this week." Offhandedly she asked, "What did he want to know about me?"

"Oh, your favorite color, what kind of flowers you like, that sort of thing. Now, I can't say more without spoiling the surprise, but it's like I told him, a man never goes wrong with red roses. Come on back. I'll show you what I had in mind for Madeline's bridal bouquet."

Summer had been on edge these last few days because Kyle was a reporter. Other than choosing his profession, he'd done nothing to warrant her distrust. In fact, except for asking her a few questions about her background, which was a very normal thing to do when people were getting to know one another, he'd done nothing except come to his brother's aid, sample a bowl of crème brulee at three in the morning and beguile her with his wit and charm over breakfast.

He'd hinted about making love, but she'd been thinking about that, too, so she could hardly chide him for it. She was beginning to like him. Summer took pride in the fact that she showed everyone common courtesy. She granted people who earned it her respect, but her affection wasn't given lightly. And she liked Kyle Merrick, truly liked him.

After consulting with Madeline over the phone, Summer finalized the order for the flowers for the wedding. Josie Rose was right. The bridal wreath spiraea, lilacs and baby's breath were going to be perfect compliments to the sprigs of apple blossoms from Madeline's family orchard. She spoke with Chelsea first and then Abby, as she started back toward her car. Since the rain had dwindled to a mild sprinkle by then, she didn't even bother with an umbrella.

She smiled a greeting to Brad Douglas, one of the accountants with the CPA firm located across the street, waved to Greg and Celia Michaels, owners of the antique store around the corner, and held out a steadying hand to Mac Bower who'd been the proprietor of Bower's Bar & Grill for sixty-five years.

A pair of strappy, high-heeled sandals in the window of the shoe store on the corner caught her eye. Lo and behold, they were even on sale.

The world felt like a very good place, indeed.

Chapter Six

The door between the kitchen and dining room was open when Summer returned to the inn late that Friday morning. As she hung her shoulder bag on the hook next to the refrigerator, she could see all the way to the parlor where Kyle was reading a magazine. He looked pretty comfortable hunkered down in an old leather chair favored by many of her guests. His elbows rested on the padded arms; one ankle balanced on his opposite knee.

She left her new shoes in her room then went to the registration desk in the foyer to check for messages. Catching a movement in her peripheral vision, she glanced up and found Kyle looking at her over his magazine.

She closed the inn's website and gave him her full attention. "Did you need something?"

"I wanted to give you these." He reached beside the chair. When he stood, he had a bouquet of flowers in his right hand.

The gesture stalled her heartbeat and invoked a sigh, for the flowers weren't red roses at all, as Josie Rose had hinted. They were daffodils, at least two dozen of them, all yellow—bright, sunny yellow, Summer's favorite color. She didn't remember walking into the parlor, but she must have because she found herself standing before Kyle, her mouth shaped in a genuine O.

He looked pleased with her response, and it occurred to her that looking pleased looked good on him.

"I have something else for you." He turned and bent at the waist, a marvelous shifting of denim over man. Just as quickly, he was upright again, and in his other hand was an ornately decorated box of Godiva chocolates.

She almost moaned. "You're very fattening to have around. Did you know that?"

"Women worry too much about their weight."

With a tilt of her head, she said, "You're saying you would date a woman who weighs three hundred pounds?"

"As long as she put it in the right places, sure."

Summer laughed out loud, and it sounded far sexier than she'd intended. After thanking him for the bouquet and the chocolates, she said, "You're a wise guy, definitely."

His grin was approving and mischievous, his posture relaxed. "I can't take sole credit for the system of analysis. It was a Merrick brother joint effort a few years back. You don't want to know what prompted it. Which reminds me. Riley said I'm to meet with you here at five to eat cake."

Well, she thought.

So.

Okay.

Something was seriously wrong with her ability to think in complete sentences, but she finally managed to say, "Someone from the bakery is bringing an assortment of sample wedding cakes here about then."

There was a nagging in the back of her mind again. What was she forgetting?

"I'll see you at five," Kyle said as he settled back into the chair and picked up his magazine.

Summer took the gifts to the kitchen where she put the flowers in water and the chocolates in the cupboard behind her baking supplies. All the while, something continued to bother the back of her mind.

What on earth could she be forgetting?

Freshening guest rooms took approximately two hours each day. Summer began on the first floor and worked her way upstairs. Being careful not to disturb personal belongings such as clothes, cameras and laptops, she straightened desks and dresser tops, smoothed wrinkles from beds and fluffed pillows. She made sure faucets weren't dripping and rugs were straightened. She also put out clean towels.

Often she listened to music and let her mind go blessedly blank while she performed these daily tasks. This afternoon, she found herself thinking about Kyle's five classifications of men. Her father and former fiancé fell into the first category. By Kyle's exposition this type was the worst, but that came as no surprise to Summer.

Since coming to Orchard Hill, she'd met a few men she considered users, several losers, a smattering of smart alecks and even a dumbbell or two. Kyle was right. The wise guys were the most entertaining. Madeline's three older brothers, Marsh, Reed and Noah Sullivan, belonged in that category, and so did Madeline's fiancé, Riley.

When Summer finished freshening the guest rooms on the first two floors, she carried her basket of cleaning supplies and another armload of fresh towels up the staircase leading to the attic apartment. She knocked to be sure Kyle wasn't inside. As she'd suspected, the apartment was empty.

Unlike the other rooms where the sheets and blankets hung on the floor, Kyle had thrown his spread loosely over the pillows. She opened the windows, freshened the bathroom and hung clean towels. Returning to the main part of the room, she rinsed out the coffee pot, pushed in a chair, then went to the bed to finish the job Kyle had started. As she fished an open novel from under one of the pillows, a sheet of paper fluttered out, landing face-up on the bed.

She picked it up automatically and couldn't help noticing her name scribbled at the top. Beneath it he'd compiled a list.

1. Baltimore
2. Merlot
3. Mackinaw Island

4. Ancient Mythology
5. Six years
6. The Orchard Inn, free-and-clear
7. Refined and educated
8. Evasive—hiding something

Suspicion reared, and the pit of her stomach pitched. Her average guests didn't make a list of perceptions and things she'd told them. In fact, this discovery was a first.

Her hand shook at the implications, the words on the paper blurring before her eyes. Making a list of things she'd told him didn't make him a thief, but Kyle Merrick was an investigative reporter. That wasn't the same as a private investigator, but it didn't mean she should trust him, either, chocolates and flowers notwithstanding.

She slid the paper into the book where she'd found it and placed the book on the nightstand as she normally would, as if she'd discovered nothing out of the ordinary. She smoothed wrinkles from the sheet, tucked in the blanket and made up the bed with her signature hospital corners. All the while, the word *ordinary* resonated inside her, for what she wanted, *all* she wanted, was an ordinary life.

From the door, her gaze strayed to the top edge of the paper peeking from the book on the nightstand. She didn't know what Kyle was up to, but finding that list was a reminder to her to remain cognizant of everything she stood to lose.

At a few minutes before five o'clock, Summer showed Betty Ryan from Knight's Bakery and Confectionary

Shoppe to the back door. Behind her, four neatly labeled miniature wedding cakes were lined up on the inn's kitchen table beside a large bouquet of bright yellow daffodils.

Several of her guests had already headed home for the weekend. In the ensuing lull, Summer called Madeline. "The cakes are here, right on schedule," she said while getting plates from the cupboard.

"I don't like asking this of you," Madeline said.

"You know I don't mind," Summer murmured. "In fact, I'm happy to do it."

"I know you say you don't mind, but I'm lying here doing nothing and you're—" Madeline burst into tears.

"And I'm about to eat cake. Madeline, what is it? What did Talya say at your appointment today? Better yet, you can tell me when I get there. I'm on my way."

"No! It was a good appointment. I don't need you to come over. I just sent Riley out. I love all of you so much, but all this hovering is making me crazy. Riley and I just had our first fight over it."

Summer paused, her hand suspended over the drawer where she kept the cake knife. While Madeline gave Summer an update on her condition and progress, Summer put forks and napkins on the table next to the dessert plates. Madeline had received good news from her nurse practitioner/midwife this afternoon. Talya confirmed that Madeline's beta levels were still elevated, a wonderful indication that she was still pregnant.

"Yesterday there was minimal spotting," Madeline said over the phone. "Today there's been none. Talya said that as long as this continues, today is my last day of prescribed bed rest. As of midnight tonight I'm relieving you of fill-in bride duties. Poor Riley doesn't know what to do with me, crying one minute, pointing my finger toward the door the next. What if he doesn't come back?"

Madeline sniffled again, and Summer's heart swelled. "Are you kidding me? He's a smart guy. He'll be back, probably sooner than you think. In fact, he's probably pacing outside in the driveway right now. You're marrying the man, Madeline. It's called for better and for worse."

"I'm afraid Riley's getting the worse first."

"Riley is getting the best, and he knows it," Summer declared.

"I hope you're right," Madeline said, sounding more like herself. "Just this morning we were talking about names…."

Laughing at Madeline's anecdotes, Summer looked around the room. Everything was ready in the kitchen. She was prepared in other ways, too. Madeline had said that as of midnight tonight, Summer would no longer be a fill-in bride. She wasn't going to wait until midnight to demonstrate a new-and-improved, friendly-but-businesslike manner with Kyle. No more shared middle-of-the-night crème brulee, no more laughing over morning coffee, no more heartrending emotion over something as sweet and simple as a bouquet of daffodils.

Her guard had slipped but she'd resurrected it. She felt a twinge of disappointment over that, for Kyle was a hot-blooded man, and he'd brought out her passionate side, too. But it was something she—

"Summer are you there?" Madeline asked.

"Hmm," Summer said.

"Summer?"

"Hmm?"

"You seem distracted."

Kyle had just entered the room. He stood in the doorway, feet apart, one hand on his hip. She could see him taking everything in, the cakes, the flowers, her.

"I'm still here, Madeline," Summer said quietly.

"Good. Kyle left a little while ago and should be arriving at the inn any minute."

"Here he is now," Summer said.

He'd showered and changed into brown chinos and a white, knit shirt. He was cleaned up, buttoned-up, tucked in. He'd even shaved. Without the whisker stubble, the lines of his jaw and chin were more pronounced, the skin above his white collar tan.

He smiled at her and let his gaze trail over her once from head to toe. The pit of her stomach did a dainty little pirouette, and she faced the fact that the return to decorum was liable to be a steep, slippery slope.

"Ready?" he asked.

She nodded.

Ten minutes later, all four cakes had been cut and Summer and Kyle had tasted each one. Twice.

"Okay," she said, doing everything in her power to ignore the expression of rapture on his lean face as he took a third bite of the first sample. "Madeline wants a simple wedding. Among other things, that means only one cake. We need to eliminate three. First, let's narrow it down. I think the one with the coconut can go."

"You're kidding." He reached around her and scooped up another forkful of that one. When his elbow accidentally brushed her breast, her heart jolted.

She drew away as if unaffected, but her body betrayed her. Rather than glance at him to see if he noticed, she said, "Coconut is one of those foods people either love or hate, which is why it's a logical choice to eliminate first."

"If you say so." He pushed the white cake sprinkled with coconut to the center of the table away from the other three. Scooping up a forkful of a light-as-a-feather white cake on the plate closest to him, he said, "I like this one."

"It's too sweet," she insisted.

"Who are you?"

Her gaze swung to him. And time suspended.

Did he know that Summer was only a nickname? Is that what he meant?

"You can't be the same woman who stood in this very kitchen eating crème brulee at three o'clock this morning."

He hadn't meant *who was she* literally.

She'd jumped to conclusions. He was joking. What a relief.

"You're sure this one's too sweet?" he said. He took another bite and held a forkful out for her to try again.

She sampled it off the end of his fork, contemplated, and nodded again.

With an exaggerated sigh, he pushed the middle cake out of the lineup. "Now we need to concentrate."

She couldn't help smiling because he made eating cake very serious work. They both tried the wedge with strawberry cream filling again, and then the chocolate-vanilla marble with the fudge filling again. And again.

"This," he said, "could take all night."

Laughing, she noticed a dab of frosting on his lower lip. Her thumb, of its own volition and without so much as a thought to decorum, glided across his mouth to wipe it away.

He caught her wrist in his hand and took the tip of her thumb into his mouth. Her heart hammered, but Summer held perfectly still. Playfulness became something else, something weightier, something living, breathing and instinctive. Her breath caught and her eyes closed, as traitorous as the rest of her.

The next thing she knew, she was in Kyle's arms. And his mouth was on hers. And everything merged, every thought converged, every heartbeat stammered, and the entire length of her body was melded to the entire length of his.

Kyle heard Summer's breath whoosh out of her, he felt her hands glide up around his neck, and he tasted the frosting they'd both sampled. None of it was enough.

He kissed her. At least that was how it began, with a kiss that exploded into something uncontrollable and invincible. It was possessive and hungry, a mating of heat and heart, discovery and instinct. Need filled him, too intense to question, and so tumultuous it became a tumbling free fall without a parachute, an adrenaline rush with only one end in sight.

He backed her to the nearest wall, his mouth open against hers, his hands all over her back. And still it wasn't enough. He molded her to him, her body soft where his wasn't, yielding and pliant where his was seeking and insistent.

Her mouth opened, and his tongue found hers. She moaned deep in her throat, the sound setting off an answering pounding in his ears, like the echoing beat of pagan drums. Slightly making room between them, he took her breast in his hand. It was full and soft and puckered and fit his hand so perfectly it was his turn to moan.

Two doors led off the back of the kitchen. He was fairly certain the first opened into a storage room. That meant the second must lead to her private quarters. He wanted to swing her into his arms and carry her there, for he needed a bed to pleasure her the way he wanted to pleasure her. And he needed it now.

He let his lips trail down her neck and loved that she tipped her head back, giving him better access. Her hands got caught in the fabric of his shirt, her touch insistent, at once strong and gentle as only a woman could be. He wanted to feel those hands on his bare skin. He wanted a lot more than that, and he would start by getting her out of her clothes.

"Summer. Are you home? Summer? Where are you?"

Kyle heard a voice in the distance. "Yoo-hoo. Summer. Jake's here." It came from far away, outside this haze of passion.

He felt the change in Summer before the words registered in his brain. She stiffened, then went perfectly still.

"I know she's here somewhere." Whoever was talking was getting closer. "I'll just be a moment. Make yourself comfortable."

Summer drew her neck away from Kyle's lips and awkwardly pressed her hand to his chest where his heart was beating hard. Through the roaring din inside her skull, she recognized Abby's voice.

She slipped out from between Kyle and the wall. She didn't have time to straighten her clothes or run a hand through her hair. She barely had time to take a shallow breath before Abby swished through the swinging kitchen door.

She stopped in her tracks the moment she saw Summer and Kyle. "Oh." Her blue eyes were round with surprise as she said, "There you are."

The feeling was returning to Summer's limbs, but the roaring in her ears hadn't lessened. "What is it, Abby?"

Upon meeting Abby Fitzpatrick for the first time, and seeing her wispy light blond hair and petite build, her bow lips and ready smile, people often assumed she was flighty. First impressions weren't always accurate, for she had an IQ that put most people to shame. It didn't require great brilliance to recognize the reason for Summer's disheveled appearance and glazed eyes, however, or the reason Kyle kept his back to the door.

"I'm sorry to interrupt," Abby said apologetically. "But Jake's here."

Summer's hands went to either side of her face. Jake. Of course. That was what she'd forgotten.

To Summer, Kyle said, "Who the hell is Jake?"

It was Abby who answered. "He's Summer's date." Her voice rose on the last word, turning the statement into a question.

Summer and Jake Nichols had been in the middle of dinner two nights ago when he'd had to make an emergency house call to help a mother goat deliver twins. He'd promised to make it up to Summer. Tonight. Summer wasn't sure what Abby was doing here, but it probably had to do with helping them choose the wedding cake.

"Shall I tell him something came—er, that you stepped out?"

"Yes," Kyle said.

"No," Summer said at the same time. She pulled a face at her friend and took a deep breath. Walking to the counter on rubbery legs, she said, "I won't lie. Tell him— What should we tell him? Tell him I'm running a little late. Can you keep him entertained for a few minutes?"

"Are you sure?" Abby asked.

The friends shared a look.

Trying on a shaky smile, Summer said, "I'm sure, Abby. Just give me a few minutes, okay?"

Abby spun on her heel and swished out the way she'd entered.

"What are you doing, Summer?" Kyle asked.

She went to the hook beside the refrigerator and opened her purse. After fishing out a brush and small mirror, she fixed her hair and applied lipstick and blush. Steadier now, she finally looked at Kyle again.

He'd turned around and now faced her. His shirt was untucked—she'd untucked it. His collar was askew, again her doing. His green eyes were stormy and narrowed, but there was little she could do about that.

She ran a hand down her dress, adjusted the waist and straightened the neckline. Taking a deep breath, she said, "I'm going to dinner."

"The hell you are."

The edge in Kyle's voice held Summer momentarily still. He walked toward her like a stealth bomber, determination and displeasure in every step. He didn't stop until he was close enough for her to see that he meant business.

"I have to go, Kyle."

"You don't have to do anything you don't want to do."

She could tell he was trying to hold on to his temper—trying but not entirely succeeding. He was a force to be reckoned with, and she understood why he was upset. She was wildly attracted to him. There was no sense trying to deny it. Her heart rate still hadn't settled back into its normal rhythm, her breathing was shallow and her legs were shaky. He'd touched her body and she'd felt his need. If Abby hadn't interrupted, they would probably be in her bedroom right now. But Abby had interrupted, and Summer did have to go tonight.

"Jake knows I'm here. I'm not going to stand him up."

He took her hand, then promptly released it. "So what we started he'll—"

Summer's chin came up a notch. A few responses came to mind, none of them nice. In the end, she met his gaze and quietly said, "Nobody else could finish what you started."

She glanced at the table beside him, and, after another calming breath, she said, "I'll ask Abby to tell Madeline we're recommending the chocolate-vanilla swirl."

Leaving the cake to dry out, and Kyle to cool off, she lifted her chin and went to greet her date.

Every bar Kyle had ever set foot in had basic similarities and a peculiarity or two that made each one unique in its own right. The three he visited in Orchard Hill were no exception. He'd knocked back a shot with his beer in the first, played a few games of pool in the second, and ordered a bar burger to go with a cold draft in the third. It wasn't the way he wanted to spend his Friday night, not by a long shot.

He'd gone up to his room after Summer left for her *date*. He had three voice mails from Grant Oberlin, each one more heated than the last, a text message from Riley, two missed calls from his mother and nothing from the source he needed to talk to. He'd tried to read, but Summer's touches in the room were everywhere, and he'd wound up pacing.

Summer insisted she wouldn't lie. That was a good

trait. But he was still mad. The answer was simple. He didn't like the thought of Summer having dinner with Jake whoever-the-hell-he-was. He liked what that dinner might lead to even less, because no matter what she insinuated she wouldn't do with anyone else, Jake whoever-the-hell-he-was was a man. Summer was a beautiful, vibrant woman, and this guy would have to be a fool not to try. Kyle had no claim on her. He had no right to feel like putting his fist in the middle of some stranger's face, either, but that didn't mean he hadn't cracked his knuckles in anticipation.

He'd dropped in on Riley and Madeline. Even in Kyle's foul mood, he could see that he'd interrupted them in the middle of making up. After that he'd driven around Orchard Hill, getting a feel for the lay of the land. There were several more bars on the strip across the river near the college. Those catered to students, and the last thing Kyle wanted to deal with tonight was a college girl.

A barroom brawl would have been a good diversion. The second bar he'd visited was a seedy dive where fights broke out with little provocation, but Kyle hadn't stayed. Sometime before he'd turned thirty, he'd learned that the pain of a split lip, a black eye and a broken hand lasted longer than the satisfaction of feeling invincible that preceded it. Though he might make an exception if he encountered Jake Whoever-the-hell-he-was.

Giving up his bar stool to some poor sap in a worse mood than Kyle, he dropped a twenty-dollar bill on the counter and left Bower's Bar and Grill. It was only nine-thirty. It was going to be a long night.

Since he'd parked his Jeep in a lot behind the second bar he'd visited, he started in that direction, in no particular hurry to get there. Most of the businesses on Division Street were closed, the storefronts emitting the blue haze of security system lighting. One window glowed bright yellow, and when Kyle went to investigate, he found himself peering into an antiquated newspaper office.

Walter Ferris was leaning on one elbow at a counter that divided the front door from the rest of the office space. Glancing up from whatever he was studying, he spotted Kyle and motioned him inside.

With nothing but time to kill, Kyle sauntered in and was given a tour of *The Orchard Hill News*. With steel desks and black telephones and an old printing press that had been retired and all but enshrined, Walter told him, when he took over the business after his father retired, it looked like something out of an old Clark Gable movie.

"You didn't tell me you were a news man," Kyle said after Walter had bent his ear for a good hour telling him about the good old days when newspapers reported real news.

Gesturing to the high ceilings and brick walls lining the interior of the building, Walter said, "She's my second-best girl. You walkin' or driving?"

"Walking, for now."

The old leather desk chair creaked as Walter lowered his tall frame into it. Motioning for Kyle to have a seat in a chair across from him, he opened a low drawer and brought out two stout glasses and a brown bottle with a crown on the label.

"Do you always work on Friday nights?" Kyle asked.

In answer, Walter opened the bottle and poured. "What I do doesn't feel like work. Used to annoy the bejesus out of Harriet." He stared into his whiskey. After swirling the amber liquid a few times, he said, "Never hurt a woman you love. Believe me, son, it isn't worth it. It'll change her forever. And that's a hard thing to live with, harder than living with the original sin."

Kyle swirled his drink, too. "You seem like a man who knows what he's talking about. How long have you and Harriet been divorced?"

"Thirty-two years." Walter picked up his glass and downed the whiskey in one gulp. Wiping his mouth on the back of his hand, he said, "I was old enough to know better, but, hell, a man isn't thinking with his brain at a time like that. Harriet and I were having problems, and my secretary was willing. Classic, isn't it?"

Kyle emptied his glass, too. "Harriet found out?"

"She knew from the start. Maybe if I'd been a little discreet she would have gone on pretending."

When Walter grew pensive and lost in his reveries, Kyle leaned across the desk, snagged the bottle and poured them both another round. "She caught you with the secretary?"

Walter brought his glass a few inches from his mouth. "In the act. In our marriage bed." He looked at the whiskey then set the drink down as if he'd lost the taste for it. "Are you surprised?"

Kyle sipped his whiskey, letting it burn his lips and tongue and throat on the way down before replying. "I have two younger half brothers and two stepmothers. After the third wife, my father stopped marrying his mistresses. Nothing surprises me."

"Where is he now, your father?"

"Sleeping peacefully beneath a maple tree in a cemetery in St. Claire. At least I hope he's at peace. The man never did like sleeping alone." Kyle capped the bottle.

"Do you hate him?" Walter asked.

"He told me I could be anything I wanted to be, and he believed it. Every summer he took all three of us boys someplace we would never forget. Sometimes it was in the middle of the wild somewhere, other times in the middle of a city. I guess you could say he had a fatal flaw, but I loved him. Luckily I didn't have to be married to him."

"And his ex-wives? Did they hate him?"

"There were a lot of catfights when I was a kid. Now that he's gone, they've formed a united front. It's Riley and Braden and me against The Sources."

Walter laughed, then his gaze followed the course Kyle's had taken.

Summer was strolling by. Kyle stared at her as if he had a radar lock on her.

She was walking next to but not touching a guy with a tattoo of an American Flag on his bicep and a Detroit ball cap on his head. She didn't look in the window, and Kyle wondered if she'd had a good time. God, he hoped not. The streetlight picked up at least five shades of brown in her hair and bleached her dress to a hue barely darker than her skin.

"It isn't much fun to watch a woman you want out with another man," Walter said.

Kyle's head turned with the speed of light. He hadn't even realized he'd made a fist of his right hand.

"Is that why Harriet flirts the way she does? Is she getting even?" he asked.

Walter put the bottle away and shut the desk drawer with a loud clank. "Harriet was a flirt before I married her and she'll likely be one until she takes her last breath. Don't get me wrong. She might dye her hair red now, but she had a redhead's fire from the get-go. She threw me out of the house the day she walked in on me. That little bitty gal dragged our mattress to the backyard and set it afire in the middle of a raging snowstorm. She filed for divorce a week later. I was belligerent back then. I showed her. I married somebody else. It was the second biggest mistake I've ever made."

"How did you two get from that burning bed to this arrangement?" Kyle asked, curious. "Any fool can see you're deeply committed to each other."

Walter's expression changed. His eyes softened, his mouth relaxed and his fingers eased on the grip he had on the arms of his chair. "She's some woman, isn't she? She forgave me."

"But I thought—"

"You thought what? That we keep separate houses? We do. I hurt her, son, the worst way a man can hurt a woman. Some women stick it out, but it changes them, and that's reality. Harriet and I made a new reality, one we can both live with. If you want Summer, find a way to make it a reality."

Kyle stood up too fast and felt a whoosh in his head.

With a chuckle, Walter said, "Come on. I'll give you a ride to the inn."

Over the legal limit, Kyle let the old newspaperman drive. From the passenger window, he watched the inn come into view. It was a handsome stone building in a historic district where the lawns were large and the houses had once been owned by the crème de la crème of Orchard Hill society. Tall and sturdy, it had a roof that looked like a top hat from here.

He wondered if Summer was back yet. He hoped she hadn't brought the vet home with her.

As Kyle opened the aging Cadillac's big door, Walter said, "Remember, son. Never hurt a woman you love."

He stood on the walkway in front of the inn until Walter had backed out of the driveway. Kyle had one foot on the first step of the front portico when it occurred to him.

Who said anything about love?

Once again the Orchard Inn beckoned Summer home.

She waited to go in until after Jake's taillights had disappeared on the other side of the bridge across the river. Above the soft silver glow of the lights on the antique posts lining her driveway, the stars were faint pinholes in the midnight blue sky. With most of her guests gone for the weekend, the windows on the second and third floor of the inn were pitch black. Only the lamp in the bay window could be seen from here.

She punched in the code on the electronic keypad, and went in through the front door. There was a knot between her shoulder blades and the start of a tension headache in her temples.

There were no medical emergencies tonight, no mares in trouble, no dogs or cats hit by cars, no iguanas falling down stairs, no parakeets suffering from apparent amnesia, or hamsters hyperventilating. As she'd listened to his marvelous stories about all those incidents—her mind wandered. Jake had known before dinner was over that she wouldn't be seeing him again. He was good about it, although not terribly happy. It would have been so much safer to care about Jake. Instead, she couldn't stop thinking about Kyle.

Abby had called Summer around eight to tell her she agreed with their choice of wedding cakes and had turned on all the usual night-lights before she'd gone home. Only one guest remained this weekend, and Abby said there had been no sign of him.

Stifling a yawn, Summer listened at the stairs. All was quiet in the old inn. Kyle's Jeep wasn't parked in the lot. Obviously he was still out. If he returned he would have to use his electronic key. Installing those locks was the first change she'd made upon purchasing the inn. It had been worth the expense for the peace of mind it gave her.

With the lamp in the window guiding her, she slowly made her way toward the back of the inn and the little apartment she kept there. The lack of sleep two nights in a row had caught up with her, and she yawned again.

Her heels clicked over the hardwood floors in the dining room. As she swung the kitchen door open, she found the room dark. She flipped the switch. And nothing. The room remained pitch black. The light must have burned out. She was forever changing lightbulbs in this old place.

She easily followed the countertop to the sink. Her fingertips were on another switch when a voice sounded behind her.

"Are you going to see him again?"

She jumped straight up as the light came on.

Heart in her throat, she spun around. Kyle sat at the kitchen table, his feet propped on a chair, eyes squinting against the sudden bright light.

Removing her hand from her throat, she said, "You nearly scared the life out of me, Kyle Merrick."

"Sorry."

He didn't look sorry. He looked lethal, like a man begging for trouble.

"So are you?" he asked. "Going to see the vet again, I mean."

Lowering his feet to the floor, he stood.

It wasn't fear that made her heart speed up. It was the expression in Kyle's green eyes, the slow, deliberate step he took toward her, and the way he reached his hand to her shoulder and gently drew her closer.

She could have stopped him at any point. He gave her time to turn away, to hold up a hand, to tell him no and mean it, but she made no sound, no movement. Her gaze remained fixed on his, her heart beating a staccato rhythm in her chest. The vein at the base of her neck fluttered up before settling down to a steady thrum.

Before either of them moved again, she knew. He was going to kiss her.

And this time, there would be no interruptions.

Chapter Seven

The light over the sink cast Summer's shadow across Kyle's chest and left shoulder. The small wedding cakes were no longer sitting on the table, and the dishes they'd used to sample them had been stacked beneath the cabinet where they belonged. Summer noticed those things the way she noticed everything, but her attention was focused on Kyle.

His face was lean and chiseled, his cheekbones hollowed slightly, his mouth open just enough to reveal the even edges of his front teeth. Beneath his gaze her fatigue and the knot between her shoulder blades was dissolving into thin air.

Awareness, brought to life out of shadows and moonlight as if just for the two of them, thrummed all around them. She'd thought the path to decorum might be a slippery slope. There was no slope; there was only this deep blue sea of possibility.

She went up on tiptoe, and sound became a strum of heartbeats, his touch stirring her longing, his arms around her a haven. His lips found hers, and suddenly they were in the center of a whirlwind, grounded in a kiss while the rest of the world spun all around them.

She had no idea where he'd been tonight, but he tasted like whiskey and burned like moonshine. There was no question in her mind about whether she was making a mistake. Some things transcended logic. She'd known, not intellectually, but instinctively, this moment was coming since the night she'd met him. She just hadn't known she'd known.

She'd become a new woman in so many ways six-and-a-half years ago. In the process, she'd begun a new life, and painstakingly learned how to be an innkeeper. At first she'd had to do a lot of pretending. She pretended nothing in Kyle's arms tonight. This was human nature in its purest form, and what she felt, felt right.

His hands went to either side of her face, levering her there as his mouth covered hers again and again. His kiss was hard and a little reckless, seeking and insistent. It filled her with so much longing she lost all sensation of time and place and reality. When his hand went to her breast, she gasped once then promptly forgot to breathe. It didn't matter. All that mattered was that he didn't stop. All that mattered was that she didn't either, that she returned his touch, pleasure for pleasure.

"Help me out here," he whispered hoarsely.

"With what?" she asked, her head tipped back, her

eyes closed, engrossed in the feel of his lips working their way down her neck.

"Where's the zipper?"

Her laugh sounded provocative and breathless. "Allow me," she whispered.

But first, she took his hand and drew him with her toward her room. Once they were both inside, he kicked the door shut, and she turned the lock.

Kyle had a hazy impression of a small suite of rooms with sloped ceilings and dark wood floors. She must have turned on the metal lamp on a table next to the bed across the room before she left. Beneath it was a black-and-white picture of three women, arm-in-arm. He was more interested in the picture Summer made, her mouth wet from his kiss, her lips full and lush, her color heightened by desire.

She was a woman, with a woman's wiles and a seductress's smile. She demonstrated both as she lowered the sneaky zipper down the *side* of her dress.

He whisked the lightweight fabric over her head, unbuttoned his shirt and peeled that off, too. He kicked off his shoes, but she was a step ahead of him. She was already barefoot, her body now covered only by the semi-transparent fabric of her bra and panties.

She held his gaze as she reached behind her and unfastened the back closure of her bra. As the garment fell away, his gaze raked down her body. Her legs were long, her panties scant. Her naval was a dip he would get to later. The delicate lower ridges of her ribs were slightly visible through her skin. Her breasts were round and creamy white and perfect.

He started there. He pressed his lips to the plump upper swells as he took them into his hands. They spilled over his palms, her nipples puckering instantly.

Her arms came around his neck, her body arching so perfectly into his. He kissed her mouth, again and again, pressing her backwards, one step and then another.

She didn't simply fall onto the bed when the backs of her knees touched the mattress. Oh no, not Summer. She turned around, threw the spread back and climbed on. The sight of her momentarily bent over in those scanty panties sent his heart rate to stroke level. His chinos landed on the floor before he'd drawn another breath.

Naked, he stretched out beside her and glided his hand along the entire length of her, his lips heating a path from her mouth to her breast and back again. Her moan of pleasure was the only music in the room, the wind against the window their only witness.

Her eyes were half-closed, as if she were learning him by heart through touch. He loved her hands on him, loved touching her in return, loved exploring and discovering what she liked, what drove her crazy and what drove her wild. Pliant and eager, she drove him wild in return.

He finally whisked her panties off. Both fully naked, they rolled across the bed, tangling the sheets and tearing out the covers as they went. He'd intended to take his time, but the blood pounding in his ears grew too insistent to be ignored, and he knew there was only so much he could do to slow this down.

She made a sound in the back of her throat. It was part demand, part plea, a request for a favor he couldn't help granting. Luckily she had the presence of mind to open a drawer in the beside table and remove a box of protection. Kyle took over from there.

Summer had been told she was beautiful in the past. Kyle said nothing with words, and yet, beneath his gaze, she felt revered. She heard foil tear, a wrapper being discarded. Then he was with her again, and it was as if the bed rose up to meet her back, and he was easing on top of her, one knee straddling her legs, his chest pressed tight to hers, his mouth on her lips.

She lost track of time then, of who moaned and who sighed. Nature had taken over, and instinct arose. He moved faster and faster, until she cried out lustily. He shuddered, and she whimpered again. It was a beautiful, noisy, raw act of possession, and it took both their breaths away.

Gradually her thoughts cleared, and her breathing ceased to be ragged. When her eyes finally fluttered open, she found that Kyle was on his side next to her, his gaze on her face. He really had the most amazing green eyes. He had a nice nose, too, for a man, and a mouth that could inspire poetry. She would have liked to continue, but she was having trouble keeping her eyes open.

She felt the mattress shift beside her, felt the sheet being drawn to her shoulders. Two nights with too little sleep had caught up with her at last.

"You never answered my question," he said after he stretched up on one elbow and reached for the chain on the lamp.

"What question?" she asked.

"Are you going to see the vet again?"

Her answer seemed to come from a great distance. "Not unless I get a dog."

Kyle chuckled in the dark. By the time he laid his head back down on the pillow, Summer was fast asleep.

He rolled over, listening to the wind and the river and the soft sound of Summer's breathing. She wasn't clingy or needy or demanding. She didn't ask to be held, and she didn't want to talk. Just the opposite, in fact. She lay on the other side of the bed, her head on her pillow, her bare thigh the same temperature as his.

With a sigh of contentment, he did something he hadn't done in more than a year. He closed his eyes and *drifted* slowly to sleep, too, a smile on his face.

Once, a few years ago, Summer had caught a miserable strain of flu that had confined her to bed for two days. It wasn't the flu that kept her here this morning. This was a fever of another sort.

She and Kyle had awakened the first time as the sun was coming up. They'd made love, slept more, and made love again. Now rays of late morning sunlight were slanting through the slats in the blinds on her windows.

Although she hadn't been completely celibate these past six years, she'd never invited a man to spend the night. She liked sleeping alone. So why did the soft rumble of Kyle's steady breathing as he slept next to her make her feel so full?

He may have been the only guest staying in the inn this weekend, but she still had eight rooms to clean, eight beds to change, and that was just the beginning. There were breakfast menus to plan for the upcoming week, and she had accounting to work on and reservations to verify and emails to answer. She needed to get up and begin her tasks, or she would never be ready when the other guests returned tomorrow evening.

Careful not to jostle him, she held in her sigh of contentment and eased to the edge of the mattress. The sheet fell away from her as her toes touched the floor.

Before she got any further, a strong arm encircled her waist. "Where do you think you're going?"

She let out a little yelp as Kyle drew her with him to the center of the bed where he fit her back to his front.

"I have an inn to run," she said, but her argument was losing steam to what he was doing to her.

He nuzzled the back of her neck with his lips, the stubble of a day-old beard making an already-sensitive area tingle. She couldn't believe he was aroused again, for they'd already made love several times.

When he'd run out of protection, she'd fumbled through a drawer until she found an unopened box. For some reason, he seemed pleased when she had to blow the dust off the top. Of course, everything she did seemed to please him.

"Chelsea, Abby and I are meeting with Madeline and the caterer this afternoon," she said. It might have made a stronger impact if her head hadn't lolled back when his hand covered her breast.

"What time?" he asked, nipping her shoulder with

his teeth while his hand continued to work magic where he touched her.

"Two o'clock."

"That's four hours from now." The deep rasp of his voice held a note of humor as he said, "We'll be cutting it close."

With a speed and agility that surprised them both, she turned onto her right side so she was facing him. Going up on one elbow, she tilted her head and arched her eyebrows. "You sound very sure of yourself."

He began to show her just how sure he was. It was a long time before either of them said another word.

This was one of those rare weekends when Summer didn't have to be careful not to use all the inn's hot water. And yet she didn't linger in the shower.

She had no reason to hurry. She had the entire place to herself, no one to answer to, two days to prepare for the coming week.

Why did she feel compelled to rush?

Kyle and Riley were meeting with Riley's tailor, and then the two of them were taking Riley's dog, Gulliver, for a run. Summer was officially off fill-in bride duty. Kyle was officially finished filling in for the groom, not that there had been a lot for Kyle to do. It was wonderful to know that Madeline was back on her feet and happy and ready to manage her remaining wedding plans. Riley Merrick had a strong woman on his hands, and, while Summer had a sneaking suspicion that it wasn't always going to make his life easy, it was exactly the kind of life he wanted.

As she dried her hair, smoothed on lotion and applied a single coat of mascara and lip gloss, a similar question played through her mind. What did she want?

She'd invited Kyle to her bed. It had seemed so natural while she'd been in his arms. Today reality was setting in.

She'd only been twenty-three when she'd arrived in Orchard Hill, and although people here saw her as worldly, she'd never been one to settle for casual sex. Though there had been nothing casual about making love with Kyle. Wild, yes, consuming and uncontrollable, definitely, but not casual.

Summer was accustomed to steering her life; she'd had no one to rely on for so long. This sensual experience was uncharted territory for her.

She doubted that was true for Kyle.

The realization gave her pause, and, in some bizarre way, it calmed her anxiety. Kyle was one of those men who exuded sex appeal. He traveled the world, and probably had exotic women slipping their room keys into his pocket on a regular basis. Surely he knew his way in and out of encounters of all kinds. Since she was out of date regarding the protocol for this kind of thing, she decided to take her cue from him.

If all they'd had was one night, so be it.

In fact, that would be best. He was a reporter who traveled the world, and she was an innkeeper who had no intention of leaving Orchard Hill. She knew better than to romanticize this. She'd stopped believing in fairy-tale endings a long time ago.

As she left the bathroom, she automatically catalogued

her surroundings. The shoes she'd been wearing last night were still where she'd toed out of them. The bed was rumpled, the sheet pulled out, one pillow on the floor.

Her gaze went to the framed photograph on the dresser. She saw that it was turned slightly, as if it had been picked up and put back down. Kyle must have looked at it.

Summer went to her dresser. Lifting the frame closer, she stared into the faces of her beloved mother and sister. She recalled her surprise upon discovering the list in Kyle's room. If he was looking for something about her past, he wouldn't find it here, for her mom and sister had died before Summer moved to Orchard Hill. Looking at their images brought a smile and left an ache. Both girls resembled their kind-natured and trusting mother, but Claire, the oldest, had been most like her. The photo had been snapped just before their mom's diagnosis. She was gone three months later. A year later Claire died, too.

Summer was glad her sister hadn't known that their father considered them pawns to be used in his business deals. At least she hoped Claire hadn't known before she'd died so suddenly of a brain aneurysm a year after their mom died from cancer. That day in a two-hundred-year-old cathedral in front of God and some of the most influential and wealthy people on the east coast, Summer had shown her father just how like him she could be. He wouldn't underestimate her again.

The media had turned her runaway bride act into a circus sideshow. It was only after she'd started over in

Orchard Hill that she'd been able to mourn her mom and sister and the life they'd shared.

Feeling melancholy, she set the photo back on the dresser and wandered from her room. She started a load of laundry then decided to work on upcoming reservations. She hadn't gotten far when her gaze homed in on a small piece of yellow paper lying on the registration desk.

How about dinner tonight?
Just so there's no confusion, now I'm officially interested.

A warm glow went through her, and a smile played across her mouth. Despite the warning bells clanging in her head, she couldn't tamp down her exhilaration. With a shake of her head and quiet chuckle, she thought, *now* he was officially interested?

If the residents of Orchard Hill wanted fine dining, they drove across the river to Dusty's English Cellar, by far the nicest restaurant in town. If it was gossip, good food, laughter and lunch they were looking for, The Hill was the perfect choice.

Summer had been meeting her three closest friends for lunch at The Hill every Saturday for six years. The décor was Americana Diner, the tables were square, the service was good, and, as usual, the place was packed.

Madeline looked radiant. Everyone who stopped by the table she was sharing with Summer, Chelsea and

Abby said so. Orchard Hill's darling beamed at each and every well-wisher.

After the last one shuffled away, Madeline whispered, "Do you think people know?"

Chelsea shook her head. Abby shrugged.

And Summer said, "I think they'll be counting backwards when the baby's born, but even then they won't know for sure. Do you care?"

Madeline beamed again. "I have morning sickness every day until eleven and the rest of the time I can't get enough to eat. I'm spilling out of my bra. Seriously, I don't even recognize my own body. I cry when it's inappropriate and I can't remember my own phone number. And yet just this morning I pinched myself because I didn't dream I could ever be this happy. I'd like to broadcast it to the world. Now, who wants dessert?"

The other three couldn't believe their ears.

"Dessert," Abby quipped. She looked good in red, her short, wispy blond hair in adorable disarray. "Are you the same person who, not twenty-five minutes ago, polished off the beef Wellington, the stroganoff *and* the stuffed chicken breast at the caterer's? Does anybody else remember hearing her say she couldn't eat another bite?"

Madeline giggled. Summer did, too. She'd been laughing a lot today. She couldn't believe the other three hadn't mentioned that. Chelsea, however, was having trouble forcing even a semblance of a smile. The reason was sitting across the room wearing a torn black T-shirt and faded jeans. Summer wondered what Sam Ralston was doing back in Orchard Hill.

Chelsea adjusted her necklace and smoothed her wrinkle-free collar, her equivalent of fidgeting. Pasting on a happy face, she signaled to the waitress to bring them all a slice of pie.

"So, Summer," Madeline said, resting her elbows on the table directly opposite Summer. "What did you and Riley talk about?"

Madeline either had cameras hidden all over town, or she really did have a sixth sense about matters of the heart. How else could she have known that her fiancé had taken Summer aside two hours ago and spoken of his concern for Madeline?

Looking into Madeline's blue eyes, Summer said, "I told him the truth. I said you're resilient and stubborn, caring and hormonal. I advised him to keep his appointment with his tailor. After all, he needs to look good for his wedding, too. I told him to enjoy a few hours away and not to worry because I've got you. Chelsea, Abby and I all do."

Emotion brimmed in Madeline's eyes all over again. Before the tears spilled over, the waitress arrived with dessert. Summer moved slightly to make room. The action must have bared the side of her neck formerly covered by her hair, because Chelsea placed a gentle fingertip over the abrasion there and quietly said, "Your date with Jake must have gone well."

Four slices of pie were forgotten as three sets of eyes narrowed speculatively.

"Dinner with Jake was okay." Summer looked at Abby, for she knew whom Summer had been kissing first.

It was Madeline who said, "Okay didn't leave whisker burn on your neck."

"That happened later, after Jake dropped me back at the inn and left."

Since they all knew there was only one guest spending the weekend at the inn, it didn't take any of them long to react. Abby covered her mouth with one hand. Chelsea's eyes widened, and Madeline put down her fork.

"Do you mean you and Kyle?" she asked.

Summer lifted one shoulder and nodded at the same time.

"Riley's *brother,* Kyle?" Madeline persisted.

"I didn't plan it, but, yes, that Kyle. Do you mind?"

The imp in Madeline had come out of hiding since she'd returned to Orchard Hill after her quest to find Riley Merrick. Summer had been surprised when her angelic friend had cut her long blond hair a few weeks ago. Yes, she was eating for two, but inside she was still the same caring girl who'd taken one look into Summer's eyes six years ago. She'd often told Summer that she'd found the sister she'd never had that day.

"Mind? I've been trying to match you up with my brothers for years. I'd love you to be my sister-in-law."

Summer held up one hand. "Nobody said anything about marriage. But you should know this is your fault."

"My fault?" Madeline quipped.

Abby and Chelsea were all ears, too.

"Remember Tuesday night when you told all of us

to close our eyes and envision the man of our dreams?"
Summer asked.

"You pictured Kyle?" Abby said.

"I dreamed of a man who was shirtless and sexy,
water glistening on his chest. Kyle arrived at the inn
that same night soaking wet."

Pushing her dessert plate back, Abby said, "I drew a
blank."

Summer noticed Chelsea looking into the distance.
Sam Ralston was staring back at her, his jaw set, his
shoulders back, arms folded across his chest as if begging for trouble.

The waitress returned to top off their coffees. "There's
a man in town asking about you, Summer," Rosy Sirrine
said.

Looking up at the iconic waitress, Summer said,
"Does he have dark hair and green eyes?"

Rosy fanned herself. "Oooeee. That's him. When
I refilled his coffee cup and gave him extra cream he
called me Aphrodite, the goddess of love. When I told
him charm doesn't work on me, he muttered something
about furies."

Summer smiled to herself, because in Greek Mythology The Furies were avenging female spirits mere
mortals feared. Rosy was tall and had broad hips and
steady hands. Nobody could remember a time when she
hadn't been the head waitress here, and yet there was no
gray in her black braid, no lines in her face. She finished
pouring the coffee and turned to leave as quietly as she'd
arrived.

"Wait," Summer called to her back. "What did Adonis ask?"

Rosy glanced at Summer over her shoulder, and for a moment her eyes looked as old as time itself. Summer knew something about nearly everybody she'd met in Orchard Hill. She knew that most men were intimidated by Abby's IQ, and she knew why Chelsea refused to give Sam Ralston the satisfaction of looking directly at him, and she knew that the couple that owned The Hill were thinking about retiring. But she knew almost nothing about Rosy Sirrine.

The older woman finally spoke. "When a body's looking for the truth, it's best to go directly to the source."

Summer got lost in her reveries as she pondered that. Kyle Merrick was an investigative reporter, and yet he'd asked her very few personal questions. She'd seen that list in his room, so she knew he was gathering information about her. The details of her past weren't buried very deep. With his investigative skills, he could have easily discovered her secrets. Why hadn't he said something or done something?

Did she have this all wrong? Was he the one hiding something? What was *his* secret?

By the time Summer turned her attention back to her friends, Abby and Chelsea had dropped their napkins on the table next to their uneaten dessert. Summer did the same.

Looking at each of her friends, Madeline said, "Aren't any of you going to eat your pie?"

At the same time, Summer, Abby and Chelsea pushed

their plates toward Madeline. Not even Chelsea could help laughing when Madeline dug in.

Summer was on the second floor of the inn when she caught her first whiff of something wonderful wafting on the air. By the time she finished her work in Room Seven, she'd identified the tangy aroma of Chinese take-out.

She went to the window. Sure enough Kyle's shiny silver Jeep was parked down below. She stood listening for footsteps overhead. Hearing nothing, she was about to walk away from the window when she noticed a movement near the river.

The lone figure of a man paced back and forth on the bank. Dark pants, dark shirt, dark hair. Even from this distance she knew it was Kyle.

Fairly gliding down the stairs, she put away her dust cloth and window cleaner and hurried past the registration desk where half a dozen small, white cartons sat waiting. She had no clear plan in mind as she pulled on a light, heathery sweater and was on the winding path leading down to the river when he stopped pacing. The leaves on the birch trees lining the banks were just beginning to uncurl from their buds, the river itself an orange and yellow reflection of the setting sun.

There was tenseness in Kyle's shoulders, a coiled restraint in the muscles down his back and legs. She wondered if whomever he was talking to on the phone was aware of how close Kyle's coiled control was to springing.

He said something. Listened. Repeated it, louder

the second time. Although she couldn't hear the words themselves, his tone was angry.

He muttered something crass and final, told whoever was on the other end what he could do with his opinion, and hurled the phone into the river with so much force it skipped three times before sinking out of sight.

The river babbled, the wind crooned and, from twenty feet behind him, Summer said, "That's one way to deal with poor reception."

Kyle turned slowly, first his head and then the rest of him.

As he stood looking at her in the gathering twilight, she witnessed a gradual change in him, as if something was dissipating like vapor into thin air.

Beneath his watchful gaze, she held perfectly still. She didn't know whom he'd talked to or why they'd argued, but she knew something momentous had just occurred.

The sun was below his shoulders now, his shadow stretching all the way to the tips of her shoes. They called her the keeper of secrets. She hadn't set out to uncover people's most intimate riddles. She'd simply listened.

That was the secret ingredient, quietude. More often than not, if she said nothing, people said something.

As she waited, she couldn't help noticing Kyle's rangy physique covered by his black pants and shirt. His eyes delved hers, and whatever she'd been thinking about seemed to have dissolved into thin air, too.

She wasn't the only one saying nothing. And it occurred to her that there was more than one option. He could tell her what had just transpired over the phone. Or he could take her inside and take her to bed.

Talk about a win-win proposition.

Chapter Eight

Kyle wondered how long it was going to take to come to terms with the fact that the black mark behind his name was permanent. He'd known this day was coming. Secretly, he'd been in denial, but the frustration and inevitability had been keeping him up nights for months. He hated having his hands tied. And he hated—

He turned his back on the river, on the setting sun and on the futility of his thoughts. And there was Summer.

The lighted kitchen window glowed a soft yellow in the distance behind her. A pontoon loaded down with a boisterous group of adults enjoying the spring evening and whatever was in their heavy-duty cooler chugged past, the rumble of the oversized outboard motor at odds with the heavy bass blasting from their radio.

When the boat was slightly downriver, he said, "I promised you dinner. I left it in the inn."

"I noticed." She shivered in her lightweight sweater.

"I hope you like Chinese," he said.

"I do."

He didn't know why he was talking about food. Probably because it was easier than talking about what had just transpired. He'd made an irrevocable decision. It had been coming for almost a year, the end of his career. He'd been fighting it, searching for a resolution or a solution. But there wasn't one, at least not one he could live with. He and his lawyer had participated in a long-distance conference with three men from the paper's legal department and Kyle's immediate boss. His former immediate boss.

He still had to call Grant Oberlin. He didn't know what he was going to say to the man. He didn't know what had possessed him to pitch his phone into the river, either, for he wasn't often given to fits of rage. If Summer had witnessed it, she didn't appear affected by it. Not questioning or judging, a quiet presence in a complicated world, she looked back at him.

She wore jeans and a sweater today. And flat shoes. And a gray shirt that was feminine but not frilly. Like her. A silver charm hung from a delicate chain around her neck; a pearl drop earring gleamed on each ear. He wondered if he dared ask her to come closer, for he wanted to cover her mouth with his, to wrap his arms around her and to lay her down right here. He wanted to bury his face in her neck and make love to her until the stars came out and the fire of his damnation was forgotten, doused as surely as his phone.

Looking at Summer, he realized that making love to her that way wasn't out of the realm of possibility. Looking at Summer, he was struck by the realization that anything was possible.

"Kyle?"

He started.

"Did you hear me?"

He hadn't, and he didn't apologize for it. He was too busy processing everything he was feeling. The bolt of sexual attraction was the easiest to identify, although that wasn't what had rendered him speechless.

He didn't question the discovery. He was in love with the woman staring back at him in waiting silence. He, Kyle Merrick, was in love. With Summer Matthews. A woman who apparently hadn't existed until six-and-a-half years ago.

"We don't have to do any of the things I mentioned," she said. "Even though it's getting cold out, and it'll be dark soon." She gave him a small smile that went straight to his heart. "We don't have to go inside. We don't have to eat or talk, and you don't have to come back to my room with me. We can stand out here all night if you want to."

In a hundred years Kyle hadn't expected to smile. It was hard to believe he'd zoned out enough to miss the fourth option.

"I'd like to," he said.

He had to give her credit for patience.

He'd never been so completely overwhelmed by circumstances out of his control *and* so certain he knew exactly what he was doing. He started toward her. "I'd like to eat, talk and take you to bed. Why don't you choose the order?"

Smiling that sexy-as-hell all-knowing woman's smile of hers, she let him take her hand. Together, they went inside. And although she didn't tell him where she planned to start, he was pretty sure she'd made up her mind.

"Oh, Kyle. Yes, yes and yes." Summer's eyes slipped closed, and she let her head loll back in ecstasy.

Eat. Talk. And then make love.

Hadn't that been her plan?

Luckily there were no other guests in the inn tonight; therefore nobody had heard all the noise she and Kyle were making. They hadn't quite gotten to her bedroom yet. When they'd first come in from the river, she thought she would light the closed sign in the window and gather up all the cartons of food and take them to the kitchen.

Eat. Talk. Then make love.

The closed sign was on, but the boxes of takeout were still sitting on the registration counter. All were opened, and several of them were half gone. What was there about this man that made her so ravenous? She'd always had a high metabolism, but this voracious appetite was for more than food.

Eat, talk and make love.

She hadn't really thought it was possible to do all three simultaneously. They talked a little while Kyle opened the cartons. They ate a little between kisses.

There had been a lot of kissing.

"Try this," she said, squeezing a bite-sized morsel of Guai Hua Shrimp with scallops between the ends of her chopsticks.

He smiled when her first attempt didn't make it to his mouth. It landed next to the registration book with a quiet plop. She thought his smile looked tired.

"I guess I should let Riley and Madeline know I'll be attending the wedding after all," he said.

Between bites of fried rice and egg rolls, he'd calmly told her that there was no longer a story waiting for him in L.A. He was officially no longer gainfully employed.

"I don't imagine being able to attend the wedding is much consolation," she said, spearing a piece of Chengdu Chicken with the tip of her chopstick.

"There's consolation, and then there's consolation," he said, unbuttoning her top button.

She put down her chopstick and held his hand in place. The kissing was good, and so was the takeout, but there was something lurking behind his eyes and beyond his touch. He had something on his mind, something he needed to say but hadn't yet managed to broach. So she waited. She wouldn't push him. She never pushed.

As she held his hand to her breastbone, she was glad he'd thought to plug his iPod into her computer. Although not so sure this was the time or place for

The Barber of Seville, at least the comic opera's lively overture covered the silence as Kyle decided where to begin.

She could tell by the way he withdrew his hand from hers that he was almost ready.

In a deep, slightly removed tone of voice, he finally said, "A year ago I received a tip that had to do with the trafficking and extortion of illegal immigrants. The source checked out. I saw the photographs of young kids and women, shoddily dressed and filthy, fear in their eyes as they were herded into a warehouse on the Lower East Side of Manhattan. The EIEO was behind me one hundred percent, and everybody knows how much power they wield in human rights' cases. The piece I wrote made the front page of *The Herald.*" He paused for emphasis. "Three hours *before* the authorities busted into an *empty* warehouse on the lower east side."

"There were no illegal immigrants being held against their will in living quarters unfit for rats?" she asked quietly.

He shook his head, and, although he leaned his hip against the desk, too, she knew he was far from relaxed.

"Someone leaked your story early?" she asked.

He nodded. "The EIEO wasn't pleased. When money I couldn't explain showed up in my bank account, things got even more interesting."

Summer moved the carton of fried rice out the way. Resting her elbow where the food had been, she faced Kyle.

When he was ready, he continued. "The paper

printed a retraction and launched the required investigation. They didn't prove anything. I couldn't prove anything, either, such as where that money came from or how that story could have been submitted without my knowledge. It came from my computer, contained my access code and my protected password. I couldn't be reached to verify. The paper had no reason to doubt me and every reason to trust me, so they ran it. It's like I told every lawyer I've talked to, I don't know who hacked in to my computer, and I don't stinking need money."

From the registration desk, the opera music swelled and Figaro boasted how clever he was. Kyle didn't say any more. He didn't have to. Summer believed there was a great deal he wasn't telling her, but the condensed version was that somebody had successfully and methodically ruined his career. Kyle couldn't prove his innocence, and the paper didn't need to prove his guilt. Democracy had been founded on the ideal that a person was innocent until proven guilty. Too often it was the other way around.

Summer looked into Kyle's eyes, and her heart turned over. He'd grown quiet again. Whoever had said it was the quiet ones you had to watch was wrong. The quiet ones were often the good ones. Kyle was one of the good ones, perhaps one of the few good men left in this complicated world.

She took a deep breath of air scented with meandering river and springtime. He breathed deeply, too, and looked at her in waiting silence. Everything inside her strained toward him.

She wanted to kiss him. She was going to kiss him, but first she pressed herself closer, her hands on his upper arms. Turning her face into his shoulder, she pressed her lips to his neck. The shuddering breath he took was more erotic than a moan.

She looked up at him, then lifted her hands to either side of his face. Raking her fingers through his coffee-colored hair, she went up on tiptoe and, pressing her mouth to his, let him know he didn't have to prove anything to her.

Her senses whirred and blood rushed through her veins. Kyle's kiss was familiar, yet it contained a new urgency, one she understood, for she felt it, too—this need to feel, to live and breathe and touch and be touched. Pagan perhaps, lusty definitely, but it was human and it was beautiful.

Their passion went from zero to sixty in an instant. Summer tugged his shirt from the waistband of his pants, giving her hands access to the bare skin of his back. She kneaded the taut muscles between his shoulders, slowly working her way lower. As the tips of her fingers delved the edge of his waistband, she felt his hands come around her back.

The next thing she knew she was bodily lifted to right where he wanted her. She wrapped her arms around his neck and hooked her ankles around his waist. Already the world was spinning.

Kyle needed more—more of Summer's sighs, her throaty moans, more of her hands on him, more of her skin uncovered.

He couldn't keep his mouth off hers, couldn't keep from seeking closer contact with every inch of her body pressed so close to his. But it wasn't close enough. It would never be enough through their clothes.

He set her on the registration counter and swept the cartons out of his way. And all the while he kissed her, their mouths open, tongues meeting, groans blending with the undulating final strains of the age-old opera.

"Now I know why I prefer dresses," he said, hindered by the barrier of her jeans.

How she managed to laugh when he was kissing her, he didn't know. But laughter trilled out of her, spilling over into the jagged hollows inside him.

"Kyle," she whispered, her mouth close to his ear.

He stopped fumbling with her jeans long enough to listen.

"I think I'll self-combust if you don't take me to bed."

She slid down his body. And darted for her room.

Kyle caught up with her just before she got there. He swung her into his arms, and they fell together onto the bed. He didn't think about what he was doing. There would be time for thinking later. Right now he had passion to burn off and the woman he loved to please.

Unlike last night, Summer didn't fall asleep immediately after she and Kyle made love. Once again they'd been wild, their movements so heated and frenzied her mind felt a little singed, even now.

She wasn't complaining. Kyle was an amazing lover.

The lamp was on, but he wasn't asleep, either. He lay on his back, she on her side, her head resting lightly on his chest, listening to the even rhythm of his heartbeat and the uneven sound of his breathing.

He was quiet, probably lost in thought.

They hadn't gotten around to finishing dinner. She would take care of the cartons on the registration desk later when she double-checked that the doors were locked.

She recalled the fit of frustration she'd witnessed by the river and everything that had come after. She understood his anger and the futility he was surely feeling. She'd once experienced very similar emotions.

She didn't believe he was guilty of indiscretions as the people in his profession claimed he was. Although he'd undoubtedly left a great deal unsaid, she distinctly recalled that he'd mentioned seeing photographs of the people being used as slave labor and worse. If there had been photographs, there must have been victims.

"Are you awake, Summer?"

She hummed an answer.

"Do you have a mentor?" he asked.

"I've never put it in exactly that context," she said, slipping her hand between his chest and her cheek where his chest hair was tickling her nose. "But I suppose I'd have to say my mentor is Rosy Sirrine."

The sound he made had a lot in common with a growl. She didn't think he'd asked because he wanted her to justify her choice, although she easily could have. The head waitress at the restaurant Summer frequented was at once ageless and as old as time. Rosy had worked and lived in Orchard Hill for years, and yet Summer had never heard anybody mention a single untoward detail of her life. She was wise and serene and seemed happy with her solitary life. She rarely offered advice, but when she did, people listened. Summer listened.

"What about you?" Summer asked. "Do you have a mentor?"

"There's a man who took me under his wing when I first started in the news business. He rode me harder and expected more from me than anybody I'd ever known. He survived a childhood on the streets of Boston and has a mouth on him that makes seasoned sailors blush. He taught me about life and sour mash whisky and women. And somehow, in the process, he taught me about integrity."

Summer tipped her head back in order to see Kyle's face. "Was he the one who showed you those photographs?"

The deep breath he took moved the entire bed. "His son did."

Her hair swished across his chest as she went up on one elbow, and emotion brimmed in her eyes and chest. "Are you and the son close?"

"I considered him my best friend."

"Did he have access to your computer and password?"

"I can't prove it." His gaze was on hers as she drew closer. She saw so much raw emotion in his green eyes. She wondered if he had any idea what an incredible man he was.

"You aren't going to tell this man, your mentor, about his son are you?"

He shook his head. "It would kill him."

She wanted to wrap her arms around him, to offer him comfort or solace, a haven in the storm. But he was reaching for her again, and, although the raw emotion hadn't waned, it shared the space with another kind of need.

Placing her hands on the sides of his face, Summer covered his mouth with hers. She made love to him, and it was more gentle than anything they'd shared before, slower and less frenzied, but no less fulfilling.

She was pretty sure he fell asleep later. They both did. When she awoke in the morning, the other side of the bed was empty.

Summer was stepping out of the shower when she heard the inn's back door open and close early Sunday morning. Kyle was back at the inn, at least. She wasn't sure he was coming back to bed.

She had slipped her arms into the sleeves of a long robe and was combing out her wet hair when he shouldered through her door. Wearing the same dark clothes he'd been wearing last night, he was windblown, his hair a mess, his face unshaven. He looked disreputable and not quite tame. There were shadows beneath his eyes, as if he hadn't slept well.

Although he didn't smile when he saw her, there was a subtle easing in the tension in his shoulders. She was glad about that.

Waving a white paper sack in his right hand and

lifting a cardboard drink tote in the other, he said, "I hope you like donuts."

"Have I struck you as a fussy eater?" She led the way through a low archway that separated her bedroom from a tiny kitchenette and living room she rarely used.

They settled into chairs around a small table. After divvying up the orange juice and coffees, he handed her the bag of donuts. Although the fact that they both chose an apple fritter wasn't lost on either of them, neither of them mentioned that they'd just discovered something else they had in common.

Seeing him looking at the small apartment where she'd lived these past six years, she said, "A man named Ebenezer Stone had the house built nearly one hundred and forty years ago. He died before it was finished and left the project and property to his half brother Josiah. Josiah knew that location was everything, and after the house was finished, he turned it into an inn on the newly established stage line between Lansing and Grand Rapids. Many inns fell into disrepair after the railroads were built. Josiah's grandson Mead Johnson had the business sense to sell a parcel of the property he'd inherited to the railroad for the sole purpose of building a train depot. The last of Ebenezer's ancestors was a man named Jacob. He and his wife, Marguerite—"

She stopped talking when she realized that Kyle had finished eating and was looking at her, an indecipherable expression on his face.

"I'm boring you to death," she said. "I'm afraid I get carried away when I talk about this place."

His eyes probed hers. "I like it when you get carried

away." He stood, but instead of reaching for her, he reached for his coffee and took a final sip. "I have to go," he said. "I need to grab a shower upstairs."

She studied his eyes but couldn't determine the reason for the change that had come over him. She stood, too, and cinched the sash of her yellow robe tighter.

"I ran into Walter Ferris at the donut shop," he said on his way through her bedroom. "He invited me to ride along while he delivers papers to businesses in nearby towns. Never promise a man anything when he offers to let you cut in front of him in the donut line."

She followed the course of his gaze around her room. The bed was unmade, their pillows rumpled, her pearl earring lying precariously close to the edge of the dresser. He glanced at the lamp that was no longer on and stood looking at the black-and-white photo underneath it.

Not one to press, she let him look. In his own good time, he turned his attention back to her and said, "Maybe later you can finish telling me about Jacob and his wife, Marguerite."

She smiled. The kiss he gave her then was a culmination of all their previous kisses. Although she felt reluctance in the big hands cupping her shoulders, he still released her.

Church bells were ringing in the distance when he went upstairs while she finished dressing. The pipes rattled slightly, an indication that somebody was indeed taking a shower someplace else in the inn.

Although she didn't hear his footsteps, when she looked a little while later, his Jeep was gone. For the rest of the day, she couldn't shake the feeling that something beautiful was coming to an end. And she couldn't quite put her finger on the reason.

Chapter Nine

At midnight on Sunday, Summer crossed her ankles and adjusted her pillows behind her shoulders. Noticing her foot jiggling again, she brought both knees up beneath the covers and opened her book to the page she'd just read.

Now. Where was she?

Painstakingly, she started over at the top.

The blinds were closed, the inn was quiet, and the coming week promised to be a busy one. Madeline and Riley were getting married in five days. Tomorrow was Madeline's gown-fitting and, on Wednesday, a bridal shower at Abby's. The wedding rehearsal was scheduled for Thursday and, on Friday, Riley and Madeline would become husband and wife. Madeline had become nearly ethereal, gliding through the remaining preparations with a serene smile and sense of calm and purpose that was a joy to witness.

Comparatively, Summer was a bundle of nerves.

She tried to refocus on the book in her hands. It had been written by her favorite author, was on all the best-seller lists and was currently being made into a movie for the big screen. The fact that she was having trouble remembering the premise wasn't the author's fault.

All but two of the inn's guests had returned hours before she'd checked all the exterior doors and retired for the night. The two remaining carpenters, who were not yet settled comfortably into their rooms upstairs, had called to tell her they would be arriving first thing in the morning.

She didn't know where Kyle was. She didn't even know if his Jeep was parked out in the lot with the other guests' vehicles, and she refused to allow herself to check.

He'd been in and out of the inn all day. Although she'd caught him looking at her a few times, he hadn't made any attempt to seek her out. She knew better than to be upset, and she wouldn't allow herself to be disappointed. Two days ago, she'd decided she would take her cue from him regarding the protocol for an affair. It was good advice, although admittedly easier said than done.

She'd made a valiant effort, though. All day long she'd been reminding herself that, for all intents and purposes, Kyle Merrick was a passing fancy. She wasn't sorry she'd met him, and she wasn't sorry she'd discovered the passion he'd brought to life for these few short days. And nights. She was glad she'd been there when he'd been coming to grips with the irrevocable circumstances that had brought about the end of his career.

Surely he had loose ends to tie up. She wasn't one of them.

What they'd had was a week of sex. Okay, it hadn't lasted an entire week, and it had been more than sex. For her, at least. They'd shared laughter and food, sunsets and moonlight, but she'd known from the start that whatever was between them had a beginning, a middle and an end.

The end was near.

With a sigh, she punched the pillow at her back and closed the novel she'd started an hour ago. There was no sense marking her page, for she couldn't remember a word she'd read.

She was reaching for the switch on the lamp when a soft knock sounded on her door. "Yes?" she said quietly.

"It's me, Summer," Kyle said.

She felt a lurch of excitement as she swung her feet to the floor. Every word of caution and every ounce of self-restraint she'd applied to this situation flew away as she turned the lock and opened the door.

Kyle stood on the other side, his shirt unbuttoned, the top closure on his chinos undone, as if he'd left his room in a hurry. He still hadn't shaved, and although he wasn't dripping wet, he looked very much as he had in her dream.

"I didn't think you were coming," she said.

Kyle didn't know how to respond to that so he said

nothing. The truth was, he hadn't intended to leave his room after he'd climbed the stairs two hours ago. He sure hadn't intended to knock on Summer's door.

It was Sunday night. She had an inn to run and secrets to keep. It thoroughly ticked him off that one of them was his.

Oh, he wasn't worried she would tell anybody. He didn't care who knew. What made him so damned angry was how little she shared with him in return. What made him even angrier was that he was mad about that.

What was wrong with him? This was the perfect arrangement. She was beautiful and smart, and warm and willing.

He wasn't accustomed to being the one wanting more.

It was bound to have happened sooner or later, but hey, the sex had been great. All day he'd been putting that in the past tense, as if it was over, done, long gone. All day he'd told himself it was time to move on. He should have barricaded the damn door.

"I'm glad you did," she said. "Come downstairs, that is."

Just like that, nothing else mattered. She was glad he was here, and Kyle faced the fact that, even if he'd barricaded the door, he would have found a way to Summer's room, into her arms, into her bed.

He stepped over the threshold and his mouth came down hard on hers, harder than he'd intended. He'd kissed her often these past several days, and every time was an indulgence. This was different. From the onset it was a rocket launch at three G's.

She was wearing some sort of pajamas, slightly bedraggled, and not intentionally sexy. Her nipples showed through the thin fabric of the top. The bottoms were a mere technicality.

He kicked the door shut and back-walked her to the bed. Their bodies melded, thighs, bellies, chests and mouths. She shuddered in his arms, warm and responsive and giving.

See? He didn't have a problem. What he had was a passion to burn off and a need to satisfy. It was the same for her. They were on even ground.

He stopped kissing her long enough to peel off her top. While she shimmied out of the bottoms, he shed the rest of his own clothes.

They fell to her bed together, her legs already going around him. She wanted him. And he wanted her. Even-steven. They didn't speak of the future. She'd always made sure of that, hadn't she?

What they did had nothing to do with the future, anyway. It had everything to do with this moment. So what he did was his damnedest to tangle the sheets and burn off this passion that somehow refused to be appeased for long.

Eventually, Kyle and Summer both stilled. She lay underneath him, catching her breath. Recovering enough to put two thoughts together took a little longer. She'd never known passion could be like this, could make her feel like this.

He eased to his side.

And she took a deeper breath.

The first word out of his mouth was "Damn."

She'd wondered when he would realize they'd forgotten about protection. It had only just occurred to her, too. "If it's any consolation," she said, still slightly breathless. "I'm on the pill."

"I don't forget that," he said. "I never forget."

She gave him a reassuring smile. "You're the first man I've slept with in a long, long time, and as long as you've always made sure to…you know…we're both okay, aren't we?"

He settled on his side, and she drew the sheet up over them.

"My father is probably turning over in his grave," he said. "God knows he had no self-control when it came to women, but he never forgot protection."

She wondered about the stern line of Kyle's lips. "Do fathers and sons really talk about that?" she whispered.

Releasing a deep sigh, he said, "My dad had a lot of faults. You could say his life lessons were a little on the tawdry side, but he had a good side, too. He was the reason Braden, Riley and I are close. The three of us grew up with different mothers, in different homes and in different circles. We started life at odds. Our father couldn't abide by that, so as soon as we were all old enough, he brought us together for a month each July. Every year, he traveled from one side of the state to the other, gathering us together. At first he rented a house on Lake Michigan. When we were older, we stretched it to six weeks and ventured farther—to Spain, to Italy and, once, to Timbuktu, but only because Riley didn't believe there was such a place. Beneath those sunny skies every summer we were simply and profoundly three brothers with the same dad. I haven't thought about that in a long time."

"Which of you is more like him?" she asked.

"Like it or not, we all ended up with a piece of him. Riley has his aptitude for architecture. My father's work is truly noteworthy. To this day, his buildings and designs are cited. Braden got his need for the thrill of the chase. Dad chased women. Braden for the most part limits his chase to boats, motorcycles and race cars. I wound up with our father's appetite. The two of us could eat our weight in just about anything."

She smiled. "I noticed. What about your mother? Do you take after her, too?"

"My mom is the most stubborn, determined and organized woman on the planet. Did I mention interfering? She never remarried, never tried to make me hate my father."

"You love her," Summer said.

"Yeah."

"What about your stepmothers?"

"My father's wives got progressively younger and smarter. If you repeat that, I'll deny it."

She laughed, and everything felt the way it had yesterday and the day before, relaxed and carefree and good. "What do the women in your family do?" she asked, curious now.

"They strategize, scheme and interfere. Oh, you mean when they're not trying to *help* one of us? My mom is an interior decorator. Her clients are some of the wealthiest and most spoiled and indignant people on the planet.

They're putty in her hands. Riley's mother is a biochemical engineer. She has her own line of makeup and skin care products. Braden's mom is an orthopedic surgeon. God knew what He was doing because my youngest brother has had more broken bones than Riley and I combined. One time Regina literally had to set Braden's broken arm with two sticks and some twine string at the bottom of the Grand Canyon."

When Summer chuckled, Kyle noticed that his heart rate was almost back to normal and his irascible mood was all but forgotten. He supposed he could attribute his improved outlook to endorphins, and those were the result of great sex. It was possible that the figure-eight pattern Summer was tracing on his chest had something to do with the reason he was thinking about doing it again.

"Now your mother and stepmothers are friends," she said, after he'd told her that he, Braden and Riley referred to their three mothers as The Sources.

"I'm in bed with a beautiful woman," he said, nuzzling her neck with his lips. "A beautiful, *naked* woman. Talking about my mother feels wrong on so many levels."

She laughed, and it sounded sexy and happy. He was contemplating covering her bare breast with his hand when something drew his gaze to the bedside table. A younger, black-and-white version of Summer smiled back at him from beneath the glass in the picture frame. In the photograph she stood arm-in-arm with two women. One was obviously her sister and the other, their mother.

"What about you?" he said, leaving his hand where it was beneath the covers, in safe territory between them. "Do you take after your mother in temperament, too?"

She followed the course of his gaze to the photograph. "In looks, I do, but my sister was most like her."

"Was?" he asked.

"That picture was taken just before my mother's diagnosis. Stage four leukemia, not even a particularly rare form. She lived three months. It wasn't nearly long enough, but she was wise and beautiful, and she used the time she had left to reminisce and tell us goodbye. My sister died without warning of a brain aneurysm a year later."

When she fell silent, he said, "And your father? Where is he?"

She answered without looking at him, her gaze still on the black-and-white photo. "He's not in the picture."

By the time Summer turned around again, Kyle was getting out of bed. They didn't talk any more. Oh, they exchanged a few polite pleasantries and a quick kiss after he dressed, but the atmosphere had changed.

Alone in her room, she couldn't shake the feeling that tonight had been a prelude to goodbye.

"Do you want to talk about it, dear?"

Summer hadn't realized her disquietude was so obvious.

Stirring a cube of sugar into her cup of tea at Summer's kitchen table on Tuesday morning, Harriet Ferris said, "God knows you've listened to me *kvetch* about

Walter often enough. What good does it do anyway? He's never going to pry himself away from that newspaper long enough to accompany me on my dream vacation to Ireland. It's like I told him. Taking me out for a green beer at the Irish pub in Hubbardston on St. Patrick's Day doesn't qualify as a trip to Ireland."

Summer couldn't help smiling at the inside joke about the nearby town whose inhabitants were mostly of Irish decent. The older woman's hand quivered slightly as she poured more steaming tea into their china cups. Although Summer didn't mention it, she knew that that little quiver annoyed Harriet to no end. With her dyed hair and painted fingernails and shoes with heels she loved so much, she'd kept herself up admirably all these years. Summer could picture her kissing the Blarney Stone in Ireland one day.

"There's a smile," Harriet said, looking at Summer over the rim of her teacup. "The first I've seen on your face since I arrived. You're ruminating on something. Believe me, I recognize the signs. If I were to harbor a guess, I'd say it has to do with that green-eyed Adonis who wandered through this kitchen on his way out a few minutes ago. He couldn't keep his eyes off you."

"He couldn't?" Summer set her teacup in its saucer and covered her reddening cheeks with her hands. She hadn't blushed since she was in the eighth grade.

"Walter's eyes are getting rheumy, but I still see fine," Harriet said. "What's wrong? Why are you so quiet today? Did you and that hottie have a lover's spat? Don't worry about singeing my ears. I could use a little sex, even if it's only vicarious."

Summer couldn't keep her eyebrows from lifting slightly.

"Come on, lay it on me," Harriett prodded.

Slowly, Summer began to talk. She told her dear old friend about the first time she and Kyle had kissed in this very kitchen and about other kisses, too, and how those kisses had led to a passion that neither of them seemed to be able to curb.

"So you've seen him naked. I knew it."

Summer stopped in the middle of her confessions and simply stared at Harriet.

"I know you're too classy to divulge the really good details, but you can't blame a girl for trying. Tell me this. How was it?"

Summer crossed her hands over her heart and sighed.

"So what's the problem?" Harriet asked.

"Well." Summer ran the tip of her finger around the rim of the delicate bone china cup in front of her. Time was spinning so fast. It was Tuesday already. Yesterday she'd accompanied Madeline to her final dress fitting. Afterward, Chelsea and Madeline had come back to the inn with Summer, where the three of them had put the finishing touches on the layout and wording for the wedding programs that would be handed to each guest at the candlelight ceremony Friday night. Kyle had taken the original program to the newspaper office for final printing. Between the time he spent with Riley and helping Walter at the office, and the time Summer spent seeing to her guests and helping Madeline with wedding plans, Summer and Kyle had seen little of one another. Except at night. Which brought her back to Harriett's question. So what was the problem?

"The first night he woke me up all night long, and the second night was pretty amazing, too. But then last night and the night before..."

Harriet set her teacup down, too. "Did he peter out on ya? Is that it?"

Summer sat up and then she sat back. "No. It's not that."

"Then what is it?"

"It's just...it was...he was different."

"No offense, dear, but has it ever occurred to you that he might have been *tired?* If you know what I mean."

Summer eyed the wise old woman.

"Men have their limits," Harriet said, twisting the purple beads at her neck. "In their defense, they have to do more of the heavy lifting in the bedroom than we do."

When she winked, Summer smiled in spite of herself.

"Sure," Harriet continued after she tottered to the counter and brought back a plate of cookies. "They like to boast that all they need is sex and supper, but, in the bedroom, we're Wonder Woman, and sometimes they're Batman, and sometimes they're Robin." She bit into a cookie. "Mmm. Macadamia-nut-chocolate-chip. My favorite. Could I get the recipe?"

Evidently the advice-giving session was over.

Summer took a cookie, too, and thought about Harriet's superhero analogy. For the rest of the morning and throughout the afternoon, she spent far too much time thinking about it and even more time wondering what had happened to change the passionate cyclone between her and Kyle into a freefall without a parachute.

Was it her imagination, or was the ground getting closer all the time?

As he had the previous two nights, Kyle knocked on her door just before midnight on Tuesday. Summer hadn't been pretending to read, and he didn't pretend he hadn't known he would end up in her room.

Whatever was happening between them, she let him in. And he definitely wasn't the Boy Wonder. Kyle Merrick was all man, all the way.

They talked, about the station she was listening to on the radio and about what he'd done that day and about the final wedding preparations and how Summer was of the opinion that she, Abby and Chelsea looked liked triplets in their matching pink bridesmaids' dresses. Every now and then, their breathing hitched, for they both had something else on their mind. It was desire, and it was there in the way his eyes closed halfway when she twirled her hair just so, and it was there in her sigh when he smiled.

What followed was another record-breaking, mind-boggling, body-tingling experience, further heightened because now each knew the other's pleasure points. He touched her all over, first through her gown and then without it. She was just as bold. They wound up on the bed, her bedspread beneath her back, his body pressed on top of hers. Coherent thought was replaced with feelings and textures.

He remembered protection this time, and she remembered the pleasure, the pure rush of joy that being with him this way brought her. When their bodies became one, it was powerful. Her heart throbbed against his and his mouth covered hers again and again. Small tremors gave way to the greatest bursting of sensations. She cried out his name and closed her eyes to the pounding certainty that every time was better than the last.

While she was in Kyle's arms, Summer believed she'd been imagining that anything was wrong. Afterwards, things fell apart a little, and conversation seemed slightly stilted, and she couldn't put her finger on the reason.

They fell asleep together sometime in the wee hours Wednesday morning, his arm around her and her leg over his. Before dawn she woke up alone.

She lay in her big bed in the dark, listening to the wind and the river and the creaking of her century-old inn. Riley and Madeline's wedding was only two days away. Kyle was staying in Orchard Hill until then. And she wondered when she'd started wishing that time didn't have to run out.

Chapter Ten

Strains of Big Band Music reached Kyle's ears as he was leaving his room on Wednesday morning. With no clear destination in mind, he slid his new phone into his pocket and followed a Benny Goodman medley down two flights of stairs.

He found Summer in the kitchen with her back to him. She glanced casually at him over her shoulder before the door had stopped swishing. He didn't know how she'd known he was there, for the music blaring from the portable stereo on the counter covered any sound he might have made.

After turning down the volume, she finished rinsing a plate before turning her attention to him. She was wearing a dress again. This one was powder blue and would have looked as fitting in the Big Band Era as it did today. The woman had class; there was no doubt about that.

"I hope the music didn't wake you," she said over "Serenade In Blue."

"It didn't."

His new phone rang, startling him. His nerves were shot to hell. He took the phone out, looked at the number, then turned the stupid thing off.

"You've spoken with your mentor?" she asked.

He considered not answering. On principal alone, he would have been justified. She was good at asking questions but not answering them and sharing bits and pieces of her past. "The one and only," he said.

He supposed the fact that she knew him well enough to surmise that he'd spoken with Grant could have been construed as encouraging. Kyle was in no mood for encouragement. He walked around the table, looked out the window, and shoved his hands into his pockets.

He'd shaved.

It was Summer's first impression when Kyle had walked into the room. Drying her hands on a kitchen towel, she studied him further. He'd showered, too, but that observation came moments later, after she'd wisely chosen to keep her distance. The bottoms of his designer jeans were frayed, as if he'd had them for a long time and wore them often. His shirt was unwrinkled, the cuffs rolled up to reveal the veins in his forearms.

"Are you hungry?" she asked.

"I could eat." There was something about him this morning, something barely leashed.

She quickly gathered up a place mat and cutlery.

Using the towel in her other hand as a pot holder, she reached into the oven and brought out the plate she'd filled for him an hour ago. "Do I dare come close enough to set this in front of you?"

There was reluctance in the easing of his scowl, but at least it lessened. "I won't bite the hand that feeds me, if that's what you're worried about."

She laid the place setting, set down the plate and arranged the cutlery around it. By the time she filled a glass with orange juice and carried it to him, he'd taken his first bite of spinach-and-sausage quiche.

She poured them both a cup of coffee but took a sip of hers from her position back near the sink. After taking another bite of the quiche, he tried the baked apples. She watched his gaze stray to her mouth. From there it was a natural progression down her body.

Something in his eyes held her still. It was a raw emotion that produced an almost tangible current. Feeling emboldened by the male appreciation she saw, she decided to broach a topic she'd never considered until she'd met him.

"What would you call...this?" she said, motioning between them.

He swallowed audibly, and said, "What would you call it?"

She swallowed, too, and she wasn't even eating. "I'd call it complicated."

He cut into the baked French toast with enough force to cut through the plate.

"Kyle, what's wrong? I mean, I know this is a horrible time for you, career-wise. I in no way wish to minimize the upheaval you're experiencing and the disappointment you surely feel."

"I'm dealing with that."

"Good. Then this isn't the worst time to bring up our—" She brought her hand up to cover the little vein pulsing at the base of her throat. "Relationship?"

He put his fork down and shoved his chair back. He was on his feet, but he didn't come closer. "I'd hardly call this a relationship."

She'd angered him. She wasn't expecting that. She'd been thinking about this for hours, and while she hadn't been able to predict his reaction to her question, she'd assumed it would prompt something closer to denial or goodbye. She'd tried to prepare herself for either of those. This felt a little like driving in fog, and she had no idea what she would find around the next curve.

"What's wrong?" she repeated.

"What could possibly be wrong? We have the perfect arrangement. Great sex, and I mean great. Great food. You're a hell of a cook. Communication leaves a little to be desired, but that's a small price to pay, right?"

She looked at him looking at her. She was bewildered.

"What's the matter, Summer? Cat got your tongue? There's a surprise, isn't it?"

"What do you mean? What are you getting at?" Okay, now she was getting angry, too. "I've been thinking about this, Kyle. About...us. I know you're going through a rough time. And you probably have no idea what you'll be doing next week, let alone in the distant future, but I was wondering if you saw this, maybe, lasting a little while."

"How long is a while?"

"Honestly?" she asked. "I care about you."

Kyle turned his back on Summer, on the evidence of what her simple declaration was doing to him. He wanted her again. And it was starting to tick him off. Keeping his back to her, he said, "Honestly, Summer?"

Something in his tone must have caused her to pause. "What is that supposed to mean?"

"Have you been honest with me? Really?" he asked.

"I haven't told you anything that isn't true."

"You haven't told me much of anything, period, have you?" He spun around, and the anger seeped out of him. In its place was a renewed sense of enlightenment. He felt calm, suddenly, because he knew exactly what he needed to do.

"You've shared the most intimate secrets of your body," he said. "We've practically burned up the sheets sharing those. I know you like pasta and wine and music. I know your friends call you the keeper of secrets. Isn't that what everybody says? Who do you confide in? Not Harriet. Not Chelsea or Abby. I bet even Madeline doesn't know your biggest secret."

"My secret?" she asked, obviously uncomfortable with the direction this conversation had taken.

Glenn Miller's "Roll 'Em" whirred from the speakers across the kitchen. How fitting.

"Yes," he said, taking first one and then another step toward her. "You know, those intricate, little, inconsequential details of your life, like your mother's name and your sister's, and where you went to college and what you did before you came to Orchard Hill. Don't you find it interesting that you told me the entire history of this inn? Ebenezer Stone was the original owner, wasn't he? After him there was Josiah and Mead Johnson and Jacob and his wife, Marguerite. You've imparted their names, but you haven't told me yours."

He let that sink in.

"I've entrusted you with my secrets, Summer." He laughed, but there was no humor in it. "And I want you. You might as well know I'm in love with you. There, another secret revealed. I've been easy, but I'm not free. Come see me when you're ready to share more than that luscious body with me. Tell me a secret, Summer."

She stared back at him in utter silence. Her hazel eyes were round, her features frozen. Even that adorable, little vein in her neck was perfectly still. He wasn't surprised she didn't say anything. A sledgehammer wouldn't have stunned her any more.

He couldn't remember the last time he'd told a woman he loved her. And he'd never told one quite like this. He'd never felt like this, had never been in love like this. That was because he'd never known a woman as infuriating and intriguing as Summer, or as illusory, either.

He couldn't have known this was going to happen when he'd left his room a little while ago. Now that it had, he was relieved to have gotten it out in the open. He'd given her an ultimatum, and, by doing so, he'd effectively drawn a line in the sand. Her response remained as big an enigma as she was.

He'd thrown a lot at her. Now the proverbial ball was in her court. It was her move.

There was nothing else for him to do but wait.

He walked jauntily out of the kitchen, leaving his uneaten breakfast on the table and leaving Summer standing in the middle of the room, her mouth gaping.

Kyle moved his beer an inch to the right of the ring it left on the table at Bower's Bar and Grill. Riley sat across from him, Walter Ferris to his left. All three were pensive.

Evidently Riley's beer was just a prop, because he hadn't even taken a sip of it. Pushing his glass out of his way, the middle Merrick brother said, "Why is it that we're damned if we do and damned if we don't?"

"Because we're m-e-n," Walter said, wiping the suds from his upper lip. "And proud of it," he stated with added vehemence.

Even Riley, who drank only rarely since his heart transplant nearly two years earlier, lifted his beer to that. He and Kyle had been quietly killing time when Walter had wandered into the bar and grill on the third block of Division Street. Evidently he and Harriet had had a spat. Kyle wasn't sure why Riley was so morose. He didn't need to know. The fact that they were willing to watch water stains form on the table in a hole-in-the-wall bar in a town of mostly strangers made a strong statement by itself.

"So what are you in for?" Walter asked.

Riley looked confusedly at the older man. "In?"

"In the doghouse."

Riley practically growled, and, in that moment, he reminded Kyle of their father. "I'll have you know I don't hover!" Riley insisted.

"Good for you," Walter said.

Rather than call Riley out on the falsehood, Kyle took another drink. Hell, Riley had been hovering all week. Madeline couldn't make a move without him asking how she was feeling or, worse, if she should be lying down. In Riley's defense, he was in love with the woman. And love made men do stupid things.

Look at him, Kyle thought. He'd had it made. He'd found a woman who practically came apart in his arms every night, a woman who had good taste in music and was a magician in the kitchen. And what had he done? He'd told her he loved her in the same breath he'd issued an ultimatum.

Tell me a secret, he'd said.

In the heat of the moment he'd felt vindicated, invincible, ten feet tall. Now, ten hours later, he wondered what he'd been thinking.

What was wrong with him?

"What's wrong with women?" Walter said, his face reddening from his jowls up. "Why do they have to be so difficult?"

"How do they do it?" Kyle asked, getting into the spirit. "How do they make us so mad our blood boils and still make us want them?"

Before the other two came up with an answer, three guys who looked almost as morose as Kyle and his table-mates came in.

Riley jumped to his feet. "What are you doing here? Is Madeline alright?"

"Relax," a muscular man sporting a day-old beard and a baseball cap said.

Another man who looked a lot like the first, only younger and rougher, shouldered his way between the other two. "If we were going to tear you limb from limb, we would have done it a few weeks ago."

It looked to Kyle as if any one of them could have gone a few rounds with Riley, if they'd been so inclined. Kyle wondered who they were.

"Madeline asked us to come on down," the third man and only blond in the group said. "Demanded is more like it." This one had the same taste in clothes as Kyle. "That baby sister of ours gets more difficult every damn day."

Baby sister? *Ah,* Kyle thought. These were Madeline's older brothers, the Sullivan men.

The billiards game in the back of the room was getting loud, and the air in the room was getting dank, just like the air in a hole-in-the-wall bar should.

"Pull up a seat," Walter said, moving his chair slightly to the left. "I just proposed a toast."

The waitress brought out three more beers and Riley performed the introductions. In almost no time, Marsh, Reed and Noah Sullivan were practically family.

"To difficult women," Walter said, lifting his beer.

Each man around the table pictured someone. Walter was thinking of a spirited redhead, Riley his newly pregnant soon-to-be bride. The Sullivan brothers had somebody in mind, too. One was blond. One was a brunette.

And one was a mistake. The woman who sauntered unbidden across Kyle's mind had hazel eyes, impeccable taste and a stubborn streak a mile wide.

Lifting his beer in a salute of sorts, Kyle said, "To lines drawn in the sand. And why it's better to be a man."

Six glasses clanked. And six men drank to that.

Glasses clanked and silverware clattered as Abby and Chelsea gathered up dessert plates and silverware. Laughter trilled and the word *thank-you* was issued a dozen different ways.

Summer was oblivious.

Dazed. Fazed. And amazed.

That summed up her frame of mind.

She'd surfaced enough throughout the bridal shower to look around Abby's living room and participate enough to keep the others from calling 9-1-1. Now, lamps were on, and golden light pooled on tabletops and spilled onto the floor where ribbons and torn tissue paper lay, forgotten. Gift bags containing everything imaginable a new bride could need were waiting near the door. Chairs were still scattered throughout the room. Every one was empty except Summer's.

Madeline's bridal shower was over, but Summer had barely noticed.

Voices carried from Abby's open bedroom door. Summer sat in the adjoining room, her head in the clouds where Kyle's voice seemed to be echoing.

I'm in love with you.

Tell me a secret.

I may be easy, but I'm not free.

The breakfast dishes were still soaking in the kitchen sink in the inn. Summer's guests had returned after a long day's work. They had exchanged pleasantries, but she couldn't recall a single word they'd said. It seemed she hadn't been able to remain focused long enough to complete anything she'd started.

She'd put on ten miles in her new shoes. And that was before she'd left the inn.

I'm in love with you, Kyle had said. *I've entrusted you with my secrets. Tell me yours.*

Guys had told her they loved her before. They might have even meant it at the time or thought they did. Nobody had made the declaration the way Kyle had, and nobody had stunned her more.

"Well?"

Summer recognized Madeline's voice.

"Just a minute. Let me get the last button fastened."

That was Chelsea's.

"What do you think we should do about Summer?"

The lilting third voice belonged to Abby.

A movement in the doorway caught Summer's attention. Madeline stood on the other side, Abby on her left, Chelsea not far behind.

Summer's breath caught. As dazed as she was, she couldn't help reacting to the vision Madeline made in her wedding gown.

The dress had belonged to her mother, who had died when Madeline was a young girl. Just this afternoon, the last of the alterations had been made. This would be the last time Madeline put the gown on before she dressed for her wedding day.

As Summer found her feet, Madeline floated closer. Since Riley was staying with Madeline, Abby was storing the gown for safe keeping until Friday. It had something to do with it being bad luck if the groom saw the dress before the wedding began. Madeline didn't believe in luck. She believed in destiny, and, looking at her—her cheeks rosy, her blue eyes shining, the dress rustling as she came closer—Summer wished she believed in it, too.

The silk had aged like fine wine, mellowing from the bright white it had been on Madeline's mom's special day to the soft, shimmering ivory of today. The gown was sleeveless, the skirt loosely gathered.

"The seed pearls were a good idea, weren't they?" Madeline asked.

Just today Jolene Monroe had finished sewing the delicate row of pearls to the gown's neckline and hem. There was no other adornment, and the effect was ethereal. Or maybe that was just Madeline.

"I think I'll pull one side of my hair up and leave the rest down." Madeline demonstrated with her right hand. "What do you think?"

Tears sprang to Summer's eyes. Abby blew her nose. Even tough-as-nails-on-the-outside Chelsea sniffled softly.

"You are going to take Riley's breath away," Summer said.

It was the perfect answer. For the perfect bride-to-be. For what would undoubtedly be a perfect wedding day.

Madeline linked her arm with Summer's and gently drew her into the circle of her friends. Summer felt surrounded and as wobbly as the newborn goat whose birth she'd witnessed last week, unable to stand on both feet. Her dear, dear friends were here, holding her up.

They'd been doing it for six-and-a-half years. A lot of people believed she was strong. Sometimes Summer thought it, too. The veil was thinning before her eyes, and she was seeing her life more clearly than ever before.

What was strong and brave about pretending to be someone else?

"Help me get out of this dress." Madeline presented the three of them with her back. "Who wants ice cream?"

Ice cream, Summer thought. She was sifting through layers of self-discovery, and Madeline wanted ice cream. It was profound and fitting, and it made Summer smile.

"Tell me you don't want pickles, too," Chelsea said.

"No, just ice cream."

Chelsea and Abby unfastened the buttons down Madeline's back and gently lifted the gown off her. Unmoving, Summer stood in the midst of them.

When she was dressed again and her wedding gown was safely and meticulously hung in Abby's closet, Madeline linked her arm with Summer's. "Are you going to talk to him?"

There was no sense wondering how she could have known.

"Kyle gave me an ultimatum," Summer said.

"Who does he think he is?" Abby declared.

"What sort of ultimatum?" Chelsea asked.

Madeline said nothing. She and her soul sister shared a long, meaningful look. Chelsea and Abby fell silent, watching the hallowed exchange.

When Summer finally spoke, she began with her response to Abby's question. "I know who Kyle is. He's a man who needs to be trusted."

Her eyes strayed to Madeline's again, for Summer realized that the real question was, *Who am I?*

Wasn't that what Kyle was asking?

There was a short answer and a long answer. Summer knew where to begin.

Kyle was a man who needed to be trusted. And she was a woman who needed to trust.

It all seemed so natural suddenly. Summer ran to Madeline and hugged her. She gave Chelsea and Abby a hug, too.

Next, she spun around and let herself out of Abby's apartment. In her mind, she was already back at the inn, gently, tentatively perhaps, finally putting her other foot on the ground.

Chapter Eleven

The stars were out when Kyle finally got back to the inn, but he didn't give them more than a cursory glance. The wind sighed and two dogs howled from opposite corners of distant neighborhoods. He dismissed those, too.

It was one o'clock in the morning, and the lamp was on in the bay window, just as he'd expected. After letting himself in with his keycard, he listened for a moment. The stately old inn was perfectly quiet. With his right foot on the first step and his right hand on the newel post, he hesitated once more.

Fixing his gaze straight ahead, he climbed the stairs. Somebody was snoring in a room he passed on the second floor. All was quiet at the top of the third. By the light of the nearby wall sconce, he took his key from his pocket and opened his door.

"My name is Serena Nicole Imogene Matthews."

Kyle jolted in the dark. He banged his elbow so hard God only knew whom he woke up, yet he still felt a smile coming on. Cradling his buzzing hand, he peered in the direction of Summer's voice.

"You smell like a brewery," she said. "I hope you're not drunk. I really don't want to have to say this twice."

She talked tough, but he heard the little tremor in her voice. His eyes had adjusted enough to make out the hazy shape of her head and shoulders at the table ten feet away.

"I smell chocolate," he said. "What are you eating?"

He heard rustling, footsteps and paper crinkling. A lamp he'd never used came on, and at last his eyes met hers. She was standing now, one hand on the back of a chair.

The ends of her hair brushed the delicate edges of the neckline of a dove gray tank, and her long skirt nearly brushed her ankles. The box of chocolates he'd given her lay open in the center of the table. He didn't see any pieces missing.

He couldn't decide what to react to first. How damn good she looked in his room. How damn good she looked, period. Or how profoundly relieved he was that she'd come. "Serena Nicole Imogene Matthews is a lot of—"

One second Summer was standing ten feet away. The next she was in front of Kyle, her fingertips over his lips, afraid that if he spoke, she wouldn't be able to.

He smelled of beer and late night breezes and peppermint. There was a dark smudge on his chin—she thought it might be ink. His eyebrows were drawn together, an indication that patience came at a price. Something about that small imperfection gave her the courage to begin.

"In every life there comes one pivotal moment so monumental and profound it becomes a reference point to everything that came before and comes after. My moment occurred six years, seven months and three days ago.

"I was born into an affluent family from Philadelphia. My father's name is Winston Emerson Matthews the *Thurd*." She exaggerated the pronunciation, and added, "His ancestry can be traced to the Mayflower. I suppose that means mine can, too.

"My sister, Claire, and I had every imaginable luxury and opportunity growing up. In the deepest vagaries of our minds, we knew that not every girl shopped for school clothes in Paris and went to London to see plays and had maids at her beck and call.

"In those circles, it's still the man of the house who makes the money and the woman who runs the household. It was our mother who took us to dance recitals and music lessons, who made certain we belonged to the right clubs and learned the proper etiquette. She was wise and kind. Everyone loved her. On nights our father wasn't home, and there were a lot of those, she often spun stories about mythological places and divinities with names we'd never heard. I wish she'd written them down because her words painted pictures of chariots blazing across the sky.

"Our father touched our lives peripherally. He doled out praise sparingly and bestowed his smiles the same way. On occasion he engaged us in conversation. I was twenty-three when I realized it was a test."

"A test of what?" Kyle asked.

Summer looked at him. Instead of answering directly, she wandered to the far side of the room where the window looked out over the backyard and the river. Staring unseeingly into the dark, she said, "When Claire was twenty-four she became engaged to a man from a family nearly as wealthy as ours.

"From the beginning, there was something about Drake Proctor that bothered me, but Claire was head-over-heels in love with him, and our mother was dying. Maybe Claire needed to love someone then.

"After Mom died, Claire threw herself into planning the wedding. Two months before her wedding day, my phone rang in the middle of the night. Claire was crying and talking out of her head. She said she had migraine, and it felt like her skull would explode. I wondered where Drake was, but I told her I was coming, hung up and dialed 9-1-1."

Kyle listened from the other side of the room. Summer opened the window, and her words seemed to flow like the river, haltingly at times, stumbling over rocks, gaining momentum as if nearing a powerful waterfall. And he knew that pivotal moment she'd spoken of would soon be revealed.

"My sister died on the way to the hospital. I held her

hand until it grew cold and my father and Drake arrived. For the next several weeks I felt my father watching me. At the time I thought he was looking for hysteria. I couldn't have been more wrong.

"One afternoon I'd curled up on a cushion in the window seat in a little alcove in a room next door to my father's office. It was a seldom-used odd little nook and contained a dainty desk and heavy velvet drapes and floor-to-ceiling bookshelves. It had been my mother's favorite room and was the only place in that monstrous house that didn't feel as empty as a crypt."

Summer could almost feel herself being transported back to that nook. Once again, it was as if she could hear the voices that had carried through the wall. The first belonged to her father; the second was Drake's. She didn't recognize the third. The tone of the conversation was serious, the words too low to be heard clearly. Summer assumed they were discussing business. After all, Drake's marriage to Claire would have merged two of the largest, privately owned companies on the east coast.

She'd known that with the merger, the company would have gone public, opening to shareholders and stocks. A great deal of money would have been made by both families, who were already decadently wealthy and didn't need any more money. She'd learned there was a fine line between need and greed. Through the wall that day she could hear her father outlining the timeline his lawyers were working under, now that the merger was a moot point. Her father was as controlling as a nobleman or a king, and he wouldn't have considered the idea of merging without the marriage between the two families.

"My son would like to talk to you about that, Simon." For the first time Summer recognized Drake Proctor's father's voice.

"With all due respect, sir," Drake Junior said, "You have another daughter."

Summer hadn't heard her father laugh often. She would never forget the sound of it then.

"I do, don't I? I couldn't have said it better myself. You have my blessing. But I'm warning you, Serena isn't as malleable as her mother and sister were. She won't look the other way if she catches wind that you frequent the red-light district and worse."

Summer didn't move. She couldn't. Her stomach pitched. Her thoughts reeled. Was that where Drake had been the night Claire died? She prayed her sister hadn't known.

She understood her father better in that moment than she had in her entire life. To him, his wife and daughters were collateral to be used in business deals, more binding than cold hard cash and far easier to manipulate and placate with trips abroad and the finest luxuries money could buy. Summer wanted to wretch, but she didn't dare for fear the men in the next room would hear.

Her father had given Drake his blessing. His *blessing*.

As the fog in Summer's brain had cleared, her spiraling thoughts had formed a united front. Suddenly she'd known what she was going to do.

When Drake sought her out a week later on the

pretense of spending time with the only other person in the world who missed his beloved as much as he did— gag—she was ready, or as ready as she could be. She sniffled and nodded and reminisced. He began stopping over, and they began spending time together.

From that day forward, she cried only crocodile tears. In a matter of weeks Drake had taken their shared grief to the next level. It required super-human acting on Summer's part to pretend that the touch of his hand on hers didn't repulse her. The first time he kissed her, she almost threw up.

Sometimes she caught her father watching her. She met his gaze unflinchingly, saying nothing.

The imminent merging of two multi-billion-dollar empires was back on schedule. In the meantime, the pre-wedding parties were lavish, the guest list the Who's Who of Philadelphia society.

Telling him it wouldn't feel right, under the circumstances, until their wedding night, she wouldn't sleep with Drake. Somehow word got out. Drake took a lot of ribbing for it. Sometimes he almost seemed to respect her for it.

Claire's wedding morning dawned crystal clear. Even though the wedding had been postponed a few months, that was how Summer thought of that day—as Claire's.

Summer's vision cleared, and she found herself staring at Kyle. Had he been this close all the while she'd been talking? Close enough to touch if she needed to touch him. Close enough to feel the heat emanating from him. Close enough to look into his eyes and continue.

"Claire's wedding day dawned crystal clear. I underwent the transformation. I was made-up, manicured, spritzed, moisturized and scented like a virgin sacrifice about to be dropped into the mouth of a volcano. I stepped into Claire's gown, let my father fasten the clasp of my grandmother's pearls at my nape, sat for the photographer, and smiled for all the bridesmaids. And then it was time."

Once again Summer felt transported back to that day. It was as if she was standing on the steps of that cathedral, the polished marble cool beneath her shoes, the light shining through the magnificent stained glass windows feeling more like stage props than evidence of a divine presence.

The music started, and her father held out his arm. She didn't recognize the woman who took it. She didn't know the woman who smiled demurely as she fairly glided to the front of the cathedral, her elaborate elbow-length veil fluttering behind her. She went through every motion with grace, poise and dignity.

She placed her hand in Drake's. She answered the bishop's questions with the appropriate responses.

And then the bishop said, "Do you Serena Nicole Imogene Matthews take Drake Elliot Proctor the Second to be your lawfully wedded husband?"

Serena Nicole Imogene Matthews stood mute.

A hush fell over the guests, all five hundred of them. The bishop cleared his throat. Drake smiled encouragingly, but his Adam's apple wobbled slightly. Every one of the bridesmaids gestured in some way, as if they believed she had stage fright. Drake's groomsmen shifted uncomfortably from foot to foot. Her father's eyes narrowed.

Summer turned to the bishop and quietly said, "Would you repeat the question, please?"

He nodded as if relieved. Finding his page in his book again, he said, "Would you Serena Nicole Imogene Matthews take Drake Elliot Proctor the Second to be your lawfully wedded husband?"

Using the stage voice she'd perfected in drama class, she looked at Drake and said, "I wouldn't marry you if you were the last man on earth."

She wrenched herself away. Leaving Drake's side in a gown that felt as if it weighed a hundred pounds, she went down the steps while half the guests were gasping and the others were asking each other what was going on.

Her father had risen to his feet in his place of prominence in the front pew. She stopped before him.

"That was for Claire." She handed him her bouquet. "These are for Mom. It looks as if you should have had another daughter."

Gathering her skirt in both hands, she started down the aisle. Cameras flashed. The photo of her dashing from the church would appear on the front page of the society section in newspapers up and down the East Coast. Her father disinherited her immediately. And then Summer was really and truly alone in the world. She would take the nickname her mother had given her when she was small, and she would stumble into a new life.

But that day, she'd walked, faster and faster and faster

down the aisle, until she was running, until all she saw in the sea of faces were eyes and all she heard was the thundering of her own heartbeat.

"I didn't stop running for a long, long time."

Kyle watched as the haze slowly cleared from Summer's eyes. She was coming back from a distant place. He wanted to say something profound, but it wasn't his to say. Halfway through the telling, he'd noticed the sliver of the moon out the window behind her. It hung as if suspended from a thread over her right shoulder. He wanted to pluck it now and place the moon in her hand, wrapping his hands around it until its glow spread all the way through her.

There had been several instances throughout her story when he thought he'd identified her pivotal moment. The first came when her mother died and, then, when Claire had. Those were life-altering circumstances, but the pivotal moment had occurred later. It hadn't happened that day when she'd walked out of that church and walked away from a life of luxury.

Her pivotal moment was that instant when she'd heard her father laugh after Proctor had said, "You have more than one daughter."

Everything prior to that was Summer's before, and everything since, her after. Kyle was experiencing a similar moment now, a moment on which the axis of his existence rested.

The way she was looking at him now made him suspect that some time had passed.

"Are you ever going to say anything?" she asked.

He wanted to swing her off her feet, to wipe the pain

from her memory. He couldn't do that. Nobody could, so he did the next best thing. He wrapped his arms around her and held her, just held her. She came stiffly into his arms. Gradually, she relaxed. That was when he felt her tremble.

When the trembling stopped, he said, "That's a good secret."

She looked up at him and rolled her eyes. "You are going to be the death of me, do you know that?"

"Yeah? I guess we're even because you're the life of me."

She sniffled, and a smile spread across her lips. "Kyle, do you think you could kiss me now?"

Summer watched Kyle react to her request. He had a way of setting his jaw just so, of not quite closing his mouth, of taking a deep breath and holding it, only to release it slowly before drawing another. His dark hair was mussed, his cheeks less hollowed than they'd been a week ago. But it was his eyes, those green, green eyes that let her know what he had in mind a moment before he took a step closer.

He made a sound deep in his throat, part growl, all male. "I think I can do better than that."

He placed a hand on either side of her face. Slowly, he brought his face down, until his features blurred before her eyes and his breath mingled with her breath.

He'd kissed her often since he'd rumbled in on a thunderclap all those days ago. But he'd never kissed her quite like this.

There was a reverence in the way he held her face in his big hands. Absorbing the rhythm of his heartbeats and the heat that was uniquely him, she brought her body closer. Gliding her hands around his neck, she sighed.

Summer didn't rush.

She didn't push for more. She didn't hurry. For the first time in her life, she felt as if she had all the time in the world.

He swung her into his arms, eventually. He lay her down, and he lay down, too. They made love in his bed, under the eaves in her century-old inn, as the sliver of the crescent moon outside the window slowly floated across the sky, silently calling in another day.

Chapter Twelve

Summer double-checked the information on the confirmation form regarding a room reservation for October. Hosanna chimed from the bell tower on the Congregational Church as it did every weekday at half past eleven. The breakfast dishes were done, two days' worth, actually, and all the beds were made except one.

She was back in Innkeeper Mode.

She'd fallen asleep in Kyle's arms last night. Luckily, her internal clock had awakened her before her other guests had stirred. Although she would have loved to linger in bed long enough to kiss Kyle awake, too, she'd eased out of bed and pulled on her clothes. Leaving him snoring softly and carrying her shoes, she'd crept down the stairs.

A quick shower, a single coat of mascara and lip gloss, clean clothes, and she was back in the kitchen. She may not have beaten the sun up, but she was ready when her guests shuffled to the table for breakfast. Rugged carpenters that they were, they acted as if they'd died and gone to heaven when she set down their plates of scrambled eggs, American fries and ham. It made her rethink the asparagus quiche she'd been planning for tomorrow.

She'd spent yesterday in a fog. Finding the courage to step up to the invisible line Kyle had drawn in the sand hadn't been easy, and yet telling him her story had released something inside her, something that had been weighing her down for a very long time.

Today she was more like a glowing comet spinning through her chores. Baring one's soul was good medicine. Baring one's body was a close contender. She smiled to herself, feeling lighter, freer and truly understood. All because she'd shared her secrets with the only man she'd ever trusted.

She needed to call Madeline and ask if there was anything she could do before the wedding rehearsal, which was scheduled to begin at six. Tomorrow Riley and Madeline's wedding would go down in history in Orchard Hill. Just a week ago, she'd dreaded the thought of history being made here. Now she was looking forward to it.

The door chimes purled. She glanced up from her computer screen as a man with silver hair and cowboy boots entered, a cigarette clamped tight between his lips. Evidently remembering his manners, he wet his fingers and put the cigarette out.

"May I help you?" she asked.

"This is The Orchard Inn, isn't it?" His accent was Boston, but not quite the one the Kennedys had made famous. This man had climbed out of his humble beginnings, though, for his shirt had cost a pretty penny and his cowboy boots several more.

"This is The Orchard Inn, yes," she said.

He studied her with brown eyes that had probably seen more than anybody knew. She wasn't afraid. For one thing, she had pepper spray behind the counter, and, for another, she knew self-defense. Besides, she considered herself a good judge of character, and first impressions counted. This man had lines beside his mouth and unwavering rectitude in his eyes.

"May I help you?" she asked again.

"I'm looking for Kyle Merrick. Is he here?"

She couldn't give out personal information. This silver-haired man undoubtedly knew that because he smiled. "I already tried his phone. He's not answering."

He was resorting to charm. She liked it. It didn't work on her, but she liked it.

Kyle saved her the trouble of explaining that to him.

"You would try to charm the spots off a leopard as he was spitting you out."

Summer and the man both glanced at the stairs. His shirt tucked neatly into a pair of unwrinkled pants and his Italian shoes planted a comfortable distance apart, Kyle stood halfway to the top.

"What are you doing here, Grant?"

Summer started. Kyle's mentor Grant?

While Kyle descended the remaining stairs, she tried to recall everything he'd told her about his mentor. It seemed as though his last name began with an O. Not O'Connor or Oliver or Orson. Oberlin. Grant Oberlin, that was it.

"Grant Oberlin," Kyle said, descending the remaining stairs and coming to a stop on the other side of the registration counter. "Innkeeper, Summer Matthews."

"I was just making her acquaintance when you so rudely interrupted. Look at you. Just getting up and it's almost noon. The life of leisure will ruin you. Turn you into a sloth. I got here in the nick of time."

Summer studied the man who'd been harder on Kyle than anybody in the business, the man who'd taken him under his wing and who'd taught him about life and women and integrity. This was the father of the man who Kyle suspected had ruined his career.

"Maybe you have nothing better to do than sleep half the damn day," Oberlin said. "But I've been up since four. I'm *bleeping* starving. 'Scuse my French," he said to Summer. Back to Kyle, he said, "There must be some place in this one-horse town where we can eat. You can say no, but I'll dog your steps until you hear me out."

There was grudging affection in Grant Oberlin's tired eyes and grudging respect in Kyle's rested ones. With the sole intention of giving them privacy, Summer excused herself and went to the kitchen.

Kyle spun her around while the door was still swishing. Before she knew what was happening, he kissed her.

One long kiss, then he turned and left, his gait jauntier than when he'd descended the stairs.

They were both smiling now. And neither had spoken a word to the other.

Kyle was almost late for his brother's wedding rehearsal.

He practically jogged to the front of the small stone church on the outskirts of Orchard Hill where Riley was standing with a group of men that included Madeline's three older brothers, Riley's future brothers-in-law. Kyle didn't see Summer, but Madeline was busy with the reverend and an older man Kyle didn't recognize who'd apparently been assigned to walk her down the aisle. Kyle remembered now. That was Aaron's father. Aaron Andrews had been Madeline's childhood sweetheart. He'd died tragically, and, by some miraculous and mysterious stroke of destiny, Riley had received his heart.

"You'll never believe who just called me," Kyle said as quietly as he could to Riley's back.

Riley turned around and stepped aside, and Kyle came face-to-face with his youngest brother. "You called me from here?"

Braden Merrick gave Kyle a bear hug.

"It's good to see you," Kyle said emphatically.

"Yeah?" Braden groused. "Riley just told me I look like something the cat dragged in."

The Merrick brothers were almost identical in height. Riley had a way of standing, his hands on his hips, feet apart, shoulders back, eyes assessing. Kyle had been told *he* looked good coming and going. The baby of the family, Braden still wore his hair too long and played too hard. If he'd ever known fear, it didn't show when he was trying to win a race.

"I thought you weren't going to make it," Kyle said.

"I thought you weren't, either."

Kyle grinned. "I came to Orchard Hill to try to talk Riley out of this."

Braden made a show of looking around the bustling church. "Looks like you made quite an impact."

That attitude was the reason the older two had ganged up on him when they were kids. Riley said, "I'm glad you're both here."

What followed was one of those awkward moments between men, when a cuff in the arm felt like too little and a handshake too stuffy and a hug too girlie.

"I'm glad I didn't miss this," Braden said, shoving his hair behind his ears. "There's a lot of potential here."

Witnessing the silent exchange between his older brothers, Braden took a step back and said, "You can't flush my head down the toilet. You've tried. Now cut me some slack. I flew all night, moved heaven and earth and drove all day to be here. How about giving me a point for that? You can introduce me to that cute little blonde with the short hair and big—" he grinned "—eyes later."

The Merrick brothers laughed in unison for the first time in months. It was beginning to look as if the wedding really would go down in history.

In every corner of the small church there was activity. Nobody was listening to anybody else, and nobody seemed sure what he or she was supposed to be doing.

Chelsea Reynolds, the official wedding planner for to-morrow's big event, was running from group to group, her notes fluttering, her normally calm demeanor in a tattered shambles.

She consulted with a middle-aged woman holding a flute and had a discussion with a teenager tuning a violin. There was a florist somewhere and a reverend who appeared even more frazzled than Chelsea.

Kyle followed directions and stood where he was told to stand. The flutist started fluting. The first bridesmaid, Abby Fitzgerald, started up the aisle, only to be told to start over, slower next time. The flute music began again.

Marsh, Reed and Noah Sullivan, who'd shared a beer with Riley and Kyle last night, took seats in the front pew. Abby finished her trek up the aisle, and then it was Chelsea Reynolds's turn. Somebody must have said what Kyle had been thinking, because the curvy brunette took a deep breath and made a conscious effort to relax her shoulders.

Then came Summer. She wore another one of her pretty dresses. It consisted of two layers of silver fabric, the hem and sleeves fluttering in a breeze Kyle couldn't feel. Nobody had to tell her to relax. Nobody had to tell her to slow down. She glided up the aisle with the poise of Cinderella at her ball.

Kyle hadn't seen her since he'd kissed her before noon, hadn't spoken a word to her all day. When her gaze met his, something passed between them, and no words were necessary.

She took her place at the front of the church opposite

him. As Madeline started up the aisle, the flute music changed to the undulating strains of a single violin. Kyle heard sniffling and rustling and murmurs and sighs. Madeline was a beautiful bride.

Kyle had another bride on his mind.

He couldn't help imagining what it had been like that day when Serena Nicole Imogene Matthews had walked down the aisle of a different church, one filled with politicians and executives and brokers and playwrights and a prima donna or two. She'd been undeniably brave that day.

Summer was just as brave today. It couldn't be easy to put a smile on her face and walk up this aisle when surely memories of that other wedding march were close at hand.

The reverend ran through the vows, the blah-blah-blahs and the do-you's. And then the flutist and the violinist played together, and Riley and Madeline rehearsed their big exit.

Kyle met Summer at the center of the aisle. As she placed her hand in the crook of his arm, she said, "Did you and Grant get everything worked out?"

"Pretty much."

They followed Madeline and Riley. Behind them the violinist broke a string, and the flutist squeaked on the wrong note.

"Where is Grant now?" Summer asked.

"He went back to New York hours ago," Kyle said, secretly hoping the music sounded better tomorrow.

Someday he would tell Summer that Grant had come to see him today because he'd figured out who had leaked Kyle's story and why. He'd offered Kyle a prestigious job with the newspaper, his newspaper. And he'd told Kyle he wouldn't blame him if he exposed his son. Kyle had said no to both.

One day he would tell her how it had felt when Grant had clasped him by the shoulder and told him he was proud of him. Right now Kyle had something else on his mind.

"What have you been doing with yourself since Grant left?" Summer asked.

He thought she sounded like a wife already.

He looked down into her eyes and said, "I've been planning my strategy. Do you have a date for the wedding?"

"For Madeline and Riley's wedding?" she asked.

"Do you know of any other wedding that's slated to go down in Orchard Hill history tomorrow?"

He caught that little roll of her eyes. "I don't have a date."

"Would you be mine?" he asked.

She looked at him as if he'd lost his mind.

"We haven't been on a proper date yet," he said. "And I think every couple should go on at least one before they get married."

Kyle had never noticed that little dimple in her right cheek. He wondered what else he would uncover during the next fifty or sixty years. "I think we should go to the justice of the peace." He gestured to all the people running around like gerbils in a science experiment. "Why would anybody choose to go through all this?"

"I don't recall saying I would marry you."

He thought he saw a ghost of a smile on her pouty pink lips. "That's why," he said, as if it was obvious, "I think this date thing is a good idea."

They were at the back of church now, and everyone was talking at once. Chelsea had cornered the poor reverend, who was now frantically taking notes. The musicians were discussing changes, and the Sullivan men were silently relieved that they weren't going to have to employ the shotgun element to this wedding after all, as if they could have forced their sister to do anything she didn't want to do.

"Are you coming back to the inn tonight?" Summer asked.

A man Summer hadn't been formally introduced to jostled one shoulder in front of Kyle's. "Riley is getting married tomorrow. It's our brotherly duty to take him out for one last hoorah."

With a flick of a gaze, Summer looked the slightly younger man over. She couldn't help smiling as she held out her hand. "I'm Summer. You must be Braden."

Ignoring his brother, Kyle leaned closer, his breath tickling her ear. "Your room or mine?"

The breeze toyed with her hair, and a smile toyed with the corners of her lips. "Both," she said.

There was a dinner following this rehearsal and toasts to be made and more plans to finalize and laughter to be savored and schedules to coordinate and wedding speeches yet to be written. The mothers were arriving in the morning. There were always surprises when The Sources rode into town. Tomorrow Riley and Madeline's wedding would go down in history in Orchard Hill as the largest and most hastily planned event anyone could remember.

Kyle and Summer were going to be a part of that history-making moment. He'd been strategizing all afternoon.

He could hardly wait for tomorrow. Tonight he was looking forward to discovering what Summer had in store for him back at the inn.

Chapter Thirteen

Anybody who happened to be walking past the old stone church on Briar Street in Orchard Hill on Friday evening would have felt the underlying excitement in the air. Not that anybody was walking by. It seemed everybody was inside waiting for Madeline and Riley's wedding to begin.

Bouquets of apple blossoms adorned the altar; more delicate sprigs were tucked into bows made of airy netting on every pew. The windows were open, letting in a current of air that seemed to carry a giggle that couldn't quite be restrained. Guests were being seated. In the vestibule, ushers were preparing to light the tapers for the candlelight ceremony. The musicians were in their designated places where the choir normally sat.

In a small room down a narrow hallway that led to

the back of the church, Madeline and her bridesmaids were nearly ready.

Chelsea put away her brushes and powders and wands. "Okay, everybody, what do you think?" she said, turning Abby toward the floor-to-ceiling mirror.

Abby looked at her reflection. They all looked. And what they saw were four lovely young women, three dressed in the palest pink and one dressed in white. Abby and Chelsea stood in front, Summer and Madeline off to the side slightly behind them.

"Not bad," Abby said, smiling at the way her light, wispy hair framed her face.

"What I want to know," Chelsea said, tucking an errant strand of her own thick, auburn hair back into her loose chignon, "is why Madeline and Summer look so rested, while Abby and I needed a gallon of concealer to hide the dark circles under our eyes."

Abby's breath caught as she said, "Because they're both in love."

Madeline beamed, and for a moment, Summer thought the ruby necklace Riley had given his bride glowed a little brighter, too. Although she said nothing, Summer didn't deny Abby's observation. She didn't want to deny it. She was in love with Kyle.

Chelsea was right, too, she thought, turning this way and that in front of the mirror. She really did look rested. She never required a lot of sleep, but last night she'd gotten more than she'd expected. She'd left a note on the registration counter for Kyle, telling him where he could find her.

She'd fallen asleep waiting for him and awoke this

morning to her clock radio playing. Kyle was fast asleep beside her. There was something poignant about the knowledge that he cared enough about her well-being not to wake her. She'd done the same for him this morning.

Other than catching a glimpse of him in his dark suit and tie a half hour ago, she hadn't seen him all day. His mother and stepmothers, brother Braden and Riley's friend Kipp were in town for the wedding. Summer wasn't the only one who'd been busy. She would see him soon, and, when they had a moment alone, she would tell him what it had meant to her to share her innermost secrets with him.

A knock sounded on the door. "Yes?" Madeline said.

A stocky man who looked a little uncomfortable in his tight collar and tie poked his head inside. "They're ready for us, Madeline."

Madeline kissed the kind man's ruddy cheek. She was ready. They all were.

They formed a procession and followed Esther Reynolds's flute music through a labyrinth of hallways and lined up as they'd rehearsed. Abby opened the double doors, and the music changed to the heavenly strains of a single violin.

Abby went first, a butterfly of a woman and Madeline's first friend. Chelsea was next, so strong on the outside, so tender underneath.

It was Summer's turn. She squeezed Madeline's hand then stepped to the doorway, her right foot poised an inch off the floor.

All eyes were on her.

Her heart fluttered, but she didn't panic, for her gaze went beyond the sea of faces, all the way to the front of church where Kyle was looking back at her. His back straight, his shoulders broad beneath his suit jacket, he stood with his brothers and another groomsman. Above his white shirt, he had the classic bone structure of the fabled gods in Greek mythology, chiseled nose and cheekbones, deep-set eyes and a poet's mouth. But he was very much a human, very much a man. Her man.

As she started toward him, her right foot must have touched the floor. Her left foot, too. She couldn't be floating. It only felt that way.

Candlelight flickered from the window ledges. Above it the weak rays of the evening sun infused the air with the hazy purple, red and gold hues of the stained glass. Summer smelled apple blossoms. And she felt—

"Serena. Over here."

She jolted and looked at the man who'd called her name. Her former name.

She blinked as a camera flashed. Only a few of the guests noticed she missed a step. Their attention had turned to the back of the church where Madeline was starting up the aisle on Aaron's father's arm.

Summer took her place at the front of the church. Chelsea and Abby both crinkled their eyebrows in silent question. She looked at Kyle, who had taken a step toward her. With one stern shake of her head, she turned her attention back to the wedding taking place.

From that moment on, Kyle didn't hear a thing. Not music. Not the shuffling of feet, not a damn word the reverend said. Riley was the one who'd had a heart transplant. Before the ceremony was over, Kyle was going to need one, too, because he was pretty sure a hole had blown through his left ventricle.

He tried to see who had snapped Summer's picture, but the weasel was hiding behind a woman wearing a big hat. Or were there others? He looked out at the sea of faces, and suddenly everyone was suspect.

He heard a throat being cleared.

Everyone was looking at him.

"Kyle?"

He glanced at Braden.

"They're waiting for the rings, man."

Oh.

Yeah.

The rings.

He fished into his pants pocket. He almost took out the wrong ring. By some stroke of luck, he managed to withdraw Madeline's and Riley's wedding bands without dropping them. As if they'd rehearsed it this way, Braden plucked the rings from Kyle's palm and handed them to Reverend Brown.

The ceremony went on around Kyle. He supposed Reverend Brown addressed the wedding guests in some sort of a sermon. Riley and Madeline undoubtedly said, "I do."

If there was more music, he didn't hear it. Summer didn't look at him again. He knew because he barely took his eyes off her.

He heard clapping. And then Riley and Madeline were walking from the church, hand in hand.

By rote, Kyle met Summer at the center of the aisle. He couldn't read her expression as she placed her hand in the crook of his arm. At the back of the church, he recovered enough to clasp his brother in a bear hug and kiss his new sister-in-law's smooth cheek.

All three of The Sources asked him what was wrong. He kissed each of them on the cheek, too. Summer stayed close to Madeline, greeting each of the guests who went through the receiving line. He kept watch for whoever had snapped her picture but saw no one now.

He lost Summer in the throngs of well-wishers moving between the church and the banquet hall next door. He caught sight of her slipping away from the crowd and finally caught up with her in a quiet little courtyard beside the church.

"I know how this looks," he said.

Summer turned around and squinted into the setting sun. Shading her eyes with one hand, she said, "Oh, Kyle, there you are."

Wait just a cotton-picking minute, Kyle thought. What was going on? Summer sounded tired but basically fine.

"I didn't call the press. I haven't told a soul."

She looked up at him, her eyes pools of gray surrounded by coal-black lashes. "I never doubted you, Kyle."

Summer watched the transformation that came over Kyle. His eyebrows came down. His chin went up a fraction. He was as handsome as she'd ever seen him in his hand-tailored suit. He smelled like the clean, brisk breeze. Once, she'd thought he was a risk. She'd been wrong.

"I didn't doubt you when that camera flashed," she said. "Why? Because the reporter in you would have dug into my background the first time your curiosity wasn't satisfied. You've known who I am since that first morning you were here, haven't you?" She hadn't realized it at the time, but it made perfect sense now. He'd known, but instead of using it against her or to further his career or redeem it in some way, he'd guarded the information. He'd wanted her to trust him with it, with her love.

The sun was sinking and the shadows were lengthening. The dread that had held his shoulders and arms rigid turned to vapor, popping like the cork on a fine bottle of champagne. What remained after the bubbles cleared was the best part. What remained was the heart of the man Summer loved.

He moved closer, his body making contact, key contact with hers, arms, chest, hips, thighs. "I knew," he said, "but if I didn't contact the press, and I *didn't,* who did?"

She started to shrug. Remembering those times throughout the years when she'd thought she was being followed, the answer became clear.

"Drake," she said.

"Proctor," Kyle said at the same time. "Your ex-fiancé knows where you are."

Summer nodded. Drake probably did know. He'd probably always known. Her father would have known, too. Any investigator could have located her. She'd changed her name, but there were records. She didn't think her father was responsible for the photographer at Madeline's wedding, though. He'd had his revenge when he'd disowned her. The last she knew, he'd married again, a much younger woman this time. He now had a new daughter to use as collateral in future business deals.

Just then a shadow flickered at the edge of the courtyard. Kyle and Summer saw a stranger in a cheap suit and with his hair slicked back start to snap a picture.

They both looked at him, bored.

He lowered his camera as if even slime balls knew when there wasn't a story to capture.

He slunk away, and Summer said, "I smell food."

The reception was beginning in the banquet hall next door. She started toward it, but Kyle caught her hand in his and simply held it.

The breeze ruffled the fabric of her pink skirt and fluttered her five shades of brown hair. This wasn't how he'd planned to do this. Some things didn't need to be planned.

Smoothing his thumb in a circle on her wrist, he gently turned her so she was facing him. Reaching a hand into his pocket to make sure the ring was still there, he said, "I've been thinking. About making a career change."

He had her undivided attention.

"It was Walter's idea, so I can't take the credit for the initial notion, but how would you feel about marrying a guy who's about to become a partner in operating a newspaper in a small college town in mid-Michigan?"

"Did you slip a marriage proposal in there some-where?" He looked into her eyes and nodded.

He took the smile spreading across her lips as a good sign. Although it might have been risky to bring up the second phase, he braved the risk and said, "I don't know how you feel about children. But if you're willing to give me a chance, I think I'd like to start filling those bedrooms in that inn of yours."

There was a hitch in Summer's breathing. What fol-lowed was the most amazing burst of possibilities. She hadn't thought about children, at least not in the context of her own. She'd always been afraid, in the back of her mind, that she was like her father: flawed. Looking into Kyle's green eyes, she saw herself the way he saw her, strong but cautious—and maybe a little wicked—but in a good way.

"You think we should turn the inn back into a house?" she whispered.

"Wasn't that what it was always intended to be?" he asked.

He reached for her other hand. Bringing both her hands together gently in both of his, he stared into her eyes. "I never thought I would find someone like you, never dreamed I could feel this way. I love you. I love the way you daydream in the middle of the afternoon and stargaze in the middle of the night. I love your courage and I love your loyalty to your friends. Let me be as loyal to you. Would you marry me, Summer?"

The next thing Summer knew, she was staring at a diamond that caught the final rays of the setting sun. Her throat felt thick and her eyes dewy as she said, "I love you, too, and I'll marry you, Kyle Merrick." He slipped the ring on her finger and she whispered, "On one condition."

He looked ready for any condition she could name.

She pushed the dark hair off his forehead. Letting her fingers trail down his face, she skimmed his lips. "Tell me a secret."

Kyle rose to the challenge and whispered in her ear.

Her breath caught and her color heightened. Nobody in the world could make her blush but him. "I wonder if anybody would miss us if we slipped away from the reception for a little while."

Taking her hand, Kyle led her toward the banquet hall, for what he had in mind was going to take longer than a little while. They joined Madeline and Riley and Chelsea and Abby and Walter and Harriet and the Sullivan brothers and Braden and Kyle's mother and his stepmothers, too. They celebrated the marriage of two special people.

They danced, and they toasted to ever after. And they ate. Everybody loved the cake, but nobody loved it more than Summer and Kyle. As the sweet frosting melted in their mouths, their gazes met. Both were thinking about how they would celebrate when they got back to the inn.

They had the same vision in the back of their minds. What they had in store was going to last for the rest of their lives.

* * * * *

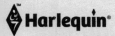
Harlequin®

COMING NEXT MONTH

Available April 26, 2011

SPECIAL EDITION®

*With an evil force hell-bent on destruction,
two enemies must unite to find a truth that turns
all-too-personal when passions collide.*

*Enjoy a sneak peek in Jenna Kernan's next installment
in her original* TRACKER *series, GHOST STALKER,
available in May, only from Harlequin Nocturne.*

"**W**ho are you?" he snarled.

Jessie lifted her chin. "Your better."

His smile was cold. "Such arrogance could only come from a Niyanoka."

She nodded. "Why are you here?"

"I don't know." He glanced about her room. "I asked the birds to take me to a healer."

"And they have done so. Is that *all* you asked?"

"No. To lead them away from my friends." His eyes fluttered and she saw them roll over white.

Jessie straightened, preparing to flee, but he roused himself and mastered the momentary weakness. His eyes snapped open, locking on her.

Her heart hammered as she inched back.

"Lead who away?" she whispered, suddenly afraid of the answer.

"The ghosts. Nagi sent them to attack me so I would bring them to her."

The wolf must be deranged because Nagi did not send ghosts to attack living creatures. He captured the evil ones after their death if they refused to walk the Way of Souls, forcing them to face judgment.

"Her? The healer you seek is also female?"

"Michaela. She's Niyanoka, like you. The last Seer of Souls and Nagi wants her dead."

HNEXP0511

Jessie fell back to her seat on the carpet as the possibility of this ricocheted in her brain. Could it be true?

"Why should I believe you?" But she knew why. His black aura, the part that said he had been touched by death. Only a ghost could do that. But it made no sense.

Why would Nagi hunt one of her people and why would a Skinwalker want to protect her? She had been trained from birth to hate the Skinwalkers, to consider them a threat.

His intent blue eyes pinned her. Jessie felt her mouth go dry as she considered the impossible. Could the trickster be speaking the truth? Great Mystery, what evil was this?

She stared in astonishment. There was only one way to find her answers. But she had never even met a Skinwalker before and so did not even know if they dreamed.

But if he dreamed, she would have her chance to learn the truth.

Look for GHOST STALKER by Jenna Kernan,
available May only from Harlequin Nocturne,
wherever books and ebooks are sold.

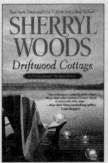 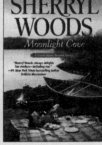 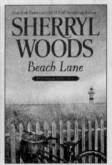